Y0-BVR-103

DARK INTRUDER

Young Kerry Derwin was perfectly contented with her carefree life in her pleasant village home. She just wanted everything to go on for ever the way it was—certainly she wasn't interested in marrying and settling down! So she wasn't best pleased when a film unit arrived in the neighbourhood and threatened to turn everything upside down. And most definitely she was not interested in the star of the film, Paul Devron. He was conceited and a ladykiller, and Kerry had no intention of adding herself to his long list of conquests! But then she hadn't actually met Paul Devron . . .

DARK INTRUDER

Nerina Hilliard

ATLANTIC LARGE PRINT
Chivers Press, Bath, England.
John Curley & Associates Inc.,
South Yarmouth, Mass., USA.

Library of Congress Cataloging in Publication Data

Hilliard, Nerina.
Dark intruder.

(Atlantic large print)
Originally published: London : Mills & Boon, 1975.
1. Large type books. I. Title.
[PR6058.I457D37 1983] 823′.914 83–2003
ISBN 0–89340–587–6

British Library Cataloguing in Publication Data

Hilliard, Nerina
Dark intruder.—(Atlantic large print)
I. Title
823′.914[F] PR6058.I45/

ISBN 0–85119–569–5

This Large Print edition is published by Chivers Press, England, and John Curley & Associates, Inc, U.S.A. 1983

Published by arrangement with Mills & Boon Limited

U.K. Hardback ISBN 0 85119 569 5
U.S.A. Softback ISBN 0 89340 587 6

DARK INTRUDER

All the characters in this book have no existence outside the imagination of the Author, and have no relation whatsoever to anyone bearing the same name or names. They are not even distantly inspired by any individual known or unknown to the Author, and all the incidents are pure invention.

CHAPTER ONE

KERRY glanced at her friend sideways. It was not a particularly sympathetic glance. Barbie, as usual, was entranced. From the look of dreamy ecstasy on her face she was in paradise. Kerry gave a mental snort.

Her eyes left Barbie's face with its expression of what she labelled vacant idiocy and went back to the screen. The man had a dark and vivid masculine attraction. An ancient Egyptian headdress of white linen bordered with gold embroidery swung against his aquiline features and the short kilted tunic and long, full cloak, also gold-bordered, could not hide the strength of his lean body. Even though he leaned negligently against a pillar, it was quite evident that he was tall. His black eyes were very slightly tilted, giving them a challenging gaiety. At the moment they also had a peculiar slumbrous fire as his glance rested on the fair-haired girl who watched him in haughty disdain from the other side of the room.

He straightened off the pillar and came towards her with panther-like grace. The expression in his eyes had deepened in a way that made Kerry decide the girl had all her sympathies—up to that point. She saw no reason at all for the idiot to give up her air of disdain for complete surrender the moment the man took her in his arms. There was all the more reason for just the opposite.

After a moment, though, she began to wriggle uncomfortably in the close confines of the seat. Love scenes always had the unhappy knack of making her feel acutely embarrassed. An envious sigh from Barbie quite finished her. She slid down in the seat and leaned an exceedingly disgruntled chin on one small and equally disgruntled hand.

'Tripe!'

It was not exactly that distinct, but her barely restrained and certainly audible snort sounded remarkably like the word. The meaning of the expression on the vivid little face was, however, quite unmistakable. Miss Derwin was bored. In fact Miss Derwin was thoroughly fed up. Her brilliant green eyes were narrowed in youthful scorn and a delightfully retroussé nose wrinkled disgustedly. A mouth that was a challenge to any man was pressed together and tilted at one corner, again in a way that would have challenged a man who guessed its cause and who retained in his veins the ancient instinct of the hunter.

The last close-up faded. The lovers, arms entwined, became one with the mists in the distance and the curtain came down. Kerry shot to her feet immediately with an audible sigh of relief. Very audible this time. She made no attempt to disguise her expression as the lights went up, nor did she let Barbie remain long in her dream world.

An unsympathetic hand reached down and fastened on the younger girl's shoulder.

'Come on, dreamy. It's finished, thank heavens,' she added caustically.

Barbara Annersley blinked and hauled her plump figure out of the seat with an assumption of comical dignity.

'You don't understand.'

'Obviously not,' Kerry retorted. 'I hope I never do, if that's the way it gets you.'

For a moment there was silence between the two. It was a friendly silence, in spite of Kerry's scathing comments. They threaded their way through the crowds leaving the cinema and came out into the bright afternoon sunlight. It always gave Kerry a slight, illogical shock to come out into daylight after seeing a film, as if night was the natural time for such an event. The sunlight too quickly brought back reality after the shrouded darkness and unreality of the cinema.

Not that she had been carried away from reality. She added the little adjuncture quickly. The dreams that Paul Devron inspired were not at all the type to sway her. The mental assurance was just a little complacent. Nonsense of that sort had no place in her life—all the eighteen years of it.

She glanced sideways at Barbie and noticed that the younger girl had fallen again into her dream state. A shade of baffled exasperation crossed her face. Not again!

'Barbie! For the love of Mike snap out of it!' She shot her friend a puzzled glance. 'How you can go so stupid over a man is beyond me.'

Barbie came out of her daze with amazing rapidity to go indignantly to the defence of her screen hero.

'He's not any man. He's Paul Devron.'

'Oh, undoubtedly,' Kerry agreed instantly, but her lips were curling again with scorn. 'Paul Devron, the idol of the silver screen, the great lover himself, the original pitter-patter of a million dreaming hearts, the . . .'

Barbie's eyes flashed. 'Kerry!' Her plump sixteen-year-old body stiffened in defence and for a moment it seemed she was prepared to defend her idol to the death, but instead she descended rather confusingly to a complete and despondent misery. 'I suppose you're right,' she agreed unhappily. 'I am a fool. Just one of millions.'

'You'll get over it,' Kerry assured her, still rather unsympathetically. 'Anyway, I don't know why you had to rush off like that to see the darn thing. You know I came into town specially to help you finish off your costume.'

Barbie turned reproachful brown eyes on her. 'I had to see the film as soon as it came on. It . . . it's the feeling he gives me,' she said, with a histrionic sweep of her hand. 'Sort of . . . of . . .'

'Yes, I know,' Kerry cut in hastily, fearing more eulogies on a subject she was beginning to cordially dislike. Barbie's constant paeans of infatuated admiration were turning her tolerant contempt of her friend's crush to actual dislike of the cause of it.

Barbie sighed and, to Kerry's disgust, the dreamy look was creeping back.

'It's like a miracle to know that he'll be coming here to Rylston.' She sighed again and this time made a vaguely prophetic gesture with her hand. 'There seems a purpose in it somehow.'

'There is,' Kerry retorted dampeningly. 'To make a film.'

Barbie ignored such crushing and logical remarks. 'They could have chosen one of the bigger towns like Exeter or Torquay, but they came to Rylston. It must mean something.'

Kerry shrugged. 'Evidently Rylston suits them more for their local headquarters. It's the closest town of any size near the moors, and as that's where they're filming, they naturally don't want to be too far away from the scene of operations.' She glanced at her watch. 'Come on, finish dreaming for now. You can gaze into his big, black eyes tonight at the ball. Right now I have to get home in time to have tea or Mallie will blow a valve!'

She quickened her steps and perforce Barbie had to as well, to keep up with her.

Although the two girls presented a strange contrast, it was one Rylston was used to. The smiling glances that met them were not ones of surprised amusement, but greeting. Both were well known, Barbie as the daughter of the local doctor and Kerry as a member of the unpredictable Derwin family that occupied the huge old rambling house on the moors, a few miles from Rylston.

Barbie gave a little skip to keep up with Kerry's longer legs. She was not really much shorter than the other girl, but quite a bit plumper. Kerry was only of medium height, but her boyish slenderness and long legs often made her look taller. Barbie's eyes were a placid blue. Kerry's were the green of dark jade and far from placid. Sometimes they sparkled with gay mischief; at others they had a decided snap of fury in them. Barbie's hair was a normal dark brown. Kerry's rioted to her shoulders in a tangled mass of vivid and almost belligerent red. It did not lie flat in sophisticated waves, but stood out in an aureole of independent, curling tendrils that were as challenging as its colour.

Barbie turned off a side street and left Kerry with a gay wave of her hand. For the time being all romantic differences of opinion were forgotten, but that did not mean that they would not be exhumed at the first possible opportunity. Kerry's views on romance were pungent and exceedingly strong, and Barbie at the moment had a one-track mind.

Alone, Kerry lengthened her stride until, except for the banner of her hair, she might really—at a first glance—have been taken for a slim youth, but the slender legs encased in the black, well-fitting jodhpurs were not those of a boy, nor was the slim waist or budding figure beneath the black tunic. Unconsciously individual as usual, she had not chosen to wear the usual type of coat with her riding kit. The neat tailored tunic, black-belted and high-buttoned to a tiny Chinese collar, gave her an air of distinction and difference from the holidaymakers who were often to be seen in riding kit in Rylston's streets. The uncommon nature of her attire and the flaming crown of her hair drew more than one masculine glance as she proceeded serenely on her way, but she was totally unaware of them. Life at that moment was beautifully uncomplicated and calm for Kerston Derwin.

The town was only small and she soon reached the end of the main street and turned off on to the road that led to the moors. Ten minutes' walk brought her to the tall iron gates that led to Rylston's riding stables, which were its main attraction.

She pushed open the gates set between walls of time-worn grey stone and swung up the gravel drive. Treveryl Hall was built of the same grey stone, merging perfectly with its surroundings. A flight of six shallow steps led up to the front door, where a tall, erect man whose brown hair was turning slightly grey was talking to a smaller wiry man.

Kerry glanced at the latter curiously. He was a stranger to her. A large American car was parked in the drive, together with a few other vehicles that she recognized as belonging to Rylstonites and yet others that probably belonged to holidaymakers. Her glance went from the large American car to the stranger, whose voice had an easily recognized accent, and she drew her own conclusions.

Colonel Treveryl turned his head and smiled at her. 'Kelvin is in the stables,' he called out.

'Thanks, Colonel.' She raised her hand in a casual little salute as she disappeared around a corner of the house, quite unaware that the American's eyes were watching her progress with a great deal of interest.

Kerry entered the large modern stables and strolled into one of the stalls with the familiarity of long custom. Kelvin Treveryl was brushing the coat of a golden mare that caught her eyes immediately. His resemblance to his father was almost startling, more than just the possession of the Treveryl dark brown hair and bright blue eyes.

He glanced over his shoulder, then as he fully caught sight of who it was, turned with a smiling wave of his hand.

'Smoky is saddled ready. I thought you'd be along about this time.'

'Thanks, Kel.' Her voice was almost absent, since her eyes were going over the mare with extreme interest. 'Joddy said you had a new mare.'

He nodded and his hand smoothed the burnished golden coat. 'Beauty, isn't she? I'll race you some time on Smoky.'

Kerry's eyes glinted. 'Done.' She added decisively: 'Make it tomorrow.'

'O.K.,' he agreed. 'Ten o'clock, Drolin Hill. Bring Rick. We'll take lunch and make a picnic of it.'

'What about Barbie?' Kerry gave him an inquiring glance and wrinkled her nose. 'She'll probably be full of idiotic dreams about Paul Devron, and it might help to snap her out of it.'

Kelvin grinned. 'I'm interested to see this Devron. Some of the rumours about him have been pretty sensational.'

'Lurid, you mean,' she retorted derisively. 'It always puzzles me how women can make such fools of themselves.'

'Being a woman yourself you can, of course, speak from great and varied experience.'

Kerry's head went up defiantly. 'You only have a couple of years' lead. And as for that type of experience, you can keep it.'

His blue eyes twinkled with friendly teasing. 'Wait until you fall in love, my child.' His tone invited comment, and Kerry did not disappoint him. Her eyes flashed green fire.

'Heaven forbid!' Then she grinned. 'If I ever show signs of it, you have my permission to duck me in the coldest and wettest water you can find.'

Knowing her well aired views on the subject, it was more than he could resist to add: 'Oh well, you might fall for Devron as well when you actually see him in the flesh.'

Kerry realized in time that she was being teased and this time did not rise, although she chuckled.

'I can imagine nothing less likely. Anyway, he's not likely to take any notice of us small fry. Merle Connors and her friends will probably hug him to themselves.' She glanced down at her watch, suddenly remembering that she was in a hurry. 'I shall have to go,' she said quickly. 'I still have to make some finishing touches to my costume.'

She turned to walk to another stall, where a smoke-grey stallion was waiting, ready saddled. The horse whinnied and nudged her softly as she came up to him. She twined her fingers in his mane and spoke to him in a crooning voice.

Kelvin wandered up to her side. 'Are you and Rick still staying here the night?'

Kerry nodded. 'Yes. Joddy will drive us in to Rylston in the Squib and pick us up in the morning.' She swung into the saddle and looked down at him from her elevated position. 'The three representatives of the Cossack regiment will meet here as arranged at eight o'clock.'

He looked up at the slim, lithe figure that sat the smoke-grey stallion with such confidence and ease, glanced at the small slender hands that held the reins with the touch of the experienced rider who loved horses, travelled upwards to the proudly held head with its flaming crown.

'You look like a Cossack already in that tunic,' he commented.

Kerry laughed. 'Whoever heard of a red-headed Cossack?'

'They will tonight,' he sent back, and there was a curiously warm smile in his eyes.

Kerry laughed again and, leaning forward, whispered something to the horse, then touched him gently with her heels.

'See you tonight.'

He watched her move out of the stables, cross the paved yard and open the gate into the paddock. Only when she had crossed the paddock and had reached the track that led on to the moors and her home did he go back inside.

There was no bus route that led anywhere near the rambling old house that was the Derwin domain. Officially it had been pretentiously named The Gables by some previous owner, but it was usually referred to by the Derwins as The House. There was a road of sorts that led in the general direction of The House, but it was a mere track and hardly suitable for motor transport. The Derwins owned a ramshackle car of ancient vintage and cranky temperament, disrespectfully labelled the Squib because of its explosive tendencies, but the younger Derwins preferred to ride the horses they loved, although there were not so many as there had been in the past. Only Kerry's Smoky and Rick's Prince occupied the once well filled stables. Richard Derwin senior, Mrs. Mallor, the old Irish housekeeper, and Joddy all preferred to use the Squib, delightfully unreliable as it was. Joddy had once had another name, but they had all forgotten it and it was probable that he himself would have forgotten to answer if addressed by it. His position in the household was rather hard to define. His duties seemed to include everything from weeding the garden to helping Mallie with the washing up, or acting as chauffeur when anybody risked their lives in the

Squib.

Rick was at present on holiday from college, where he was studying architecture, and just lately Kerry had started to give thought to some sort of career of her own. At the moment, though, such thoughts were still nebulous and vague.

Richard Derwin had once been a concert pianist, until an accident to one of his hands had finished his career. He had taken it with a very good grace and astonished his family by taking up writing detective stories that quite often were published, but the income from that source would never have been sufficient if it had not been helped out by a small private income.

Margaret Derwin had died when the twins were born. She was known to her son and daughter only as a large framed photograph that hung in their father's study and another in her practice room upstairs. She had a promising career as a ballet dancer when she met Richard Derwin, but had given it up unhesitatingly on her marriage. Her husband had taken her death badly for a time, but although he was completely devoid of business acumen, he was a very level-headed man. He had pulled himself together and proceeded to devote himself to bringing up the son and daughter she left behind. He had never put anyone in her place and always at The House there was the sense of a fourth Derwin there, invisible and silent, yet filling the old building with a sense of warmth. There was not much money at The House, but it was a happy household. Rylston knew it well and having managed to get used to a certain delightful uncertainty about the place, liked it well too.

The town itself was small and compact, a delightful mingling of the old and the new. Once it had been just another little moorland village, but a hardworking and progressive town council had enlarged and made it into a fairly popular holiday town, without spoiling any of its natural attraction. During winter it went back to being a sleepy little village, but in the summer it came alive with a gay spirit that was infectious. Its principal attraction was the Treveryl stables and the wild, beautiful scenery of the moors. For those who preferred other forms of entertainment, there was a cinema that changed its programme twice weekly, a dance every evening at the large modern hall specially built for the purpose, tennis courts, swimming pool and even a skating rink for the bolder spirits. Apart from the principal holiday attractions, there was the Rylston Social Club, home of every local affair, including the annual fancy dress carnival. Principally for Rylston's permanent inhabitants and those of the surrounding moors, it also attracted the holidaymakers.

Kerry rode home to dress for the current one.

Then an American film company arrived to swell the already crowded town. They had taken over all available space at hotels and guest houses. Some of them had even been invited to stay at private homes. The majority of the female population of Rylston (with one notable exception) had been delighted to find that one of the stars of the film was Paul Devron and the male population (single ones openly, married ones secretly) equally delighted to discover that his leading lady in the current film was the beautiful Valma Kent, the fair-haired girl who had earned Kerry's scorn by melting in his arms. The organizer of the carnival had persuaded the two stars to make a brief appearance to present the prizes for the most original costumes. Some mysterious raffle had also been arranged by Merle Connors, the daughter of Rylston's leading socialite. They had all been asked to keep their numbered entrance tickets, but what the prize was to be nobody had yet been able to discover.

Kerry had not bothered to try and find anything original for her costume. Rick and Kelvin had decided to go as Cossacks. The Derwin household could not afford luxuries like fancy dress costumes and the Cossack uniforms could be borrowed from the local dramatic society. Kerry promptly decided that there would be three Cossacks, seeing distinct possibilities in the costumes.

As she rode the sky darkened. The sun sank in a blaze of colour behind the low purple hills. She had always been a good rider, but now, in her hurry, she seemed part of her horse, a young Diana who did not know that she had an audience.

In the setting sun the weary members of the film company were packing up, ready to return to Rylston. The short, wiry man she had seen talking to Colonel Treveryl had reached the film set just prior to her passing some distance away. There was quite a reasonable road to Rylston at that point and she had stayed some time talking to Kelvin. By car he had easily beaten her to the camp and arrived in time to see the spectacular moment of her passing.

He caught sight of her just as he climbed out of the car and involuntarily glanced over his shoulder and called out:

'Paul!'

Someone moved behind him with the lithe, feline grace of a panther. A man stood at his side, tall, black-haired, with intensely dark eyes. Paul Devron did not need his attention directed. There was appreciative speculation on his aquiline features as he followed the other man's pointing hand.

Silhouetted against the setting sun and the dark shadows of a nearby hilltop, horse and rider seemed one, plunging down the steep incline to be too quickly out of sight. It was like a glimpse of a younger, primitive Earth, when Diana herself rode to the hunt, limed in the soft rays of her brother Apollo. But too soon gone, leaving behind a sense of loss, a sensation of for one moment having looked through a veil of enchantment and unreality.

And those that dealt in enchantment and unreality felt it and knew the sense of loss when it was gone.

The wiry little director drew an involuntary quick breath. 'What a shot that would have made!'

'Things like that are not arranged, Tom. They come by accident.'

Tom Marriott turned away with a shrug. 'I guess so.' He paused and then added thoughtfully, 'I wonder if it was the girl I saw at Treveryl's place.'

One dark brow went up interrogatively. 'What girl?' The voice was uninterested, even bored, as if the man merely made a conventional inquiry.

'The most striking redhead I've ever seen.' Marriott at least was enthusiastic. 'She was dressed entirely in black and her hair was like a flame against it.'

'She probably knows the effect it has.' The cynicism that was in Paul Devron's eyes had reached his voice, as if the subject of women was one that called forth disillusioned amusement.

'Perhaps.' Marriott went silent again, rubbing his chin absently. 'She would be ideal for the part of Metani.'

Devron shrugged again. 'That's your business, if you think she's suitable. You'll have to replace Rita Lane some time. Your redhead will probably jump at the chance.'

'I wonder?' He frowned slightly. 'I'll have to find out who she is. Colonel Treveryl should know.'

'What if your redhead won't agree?' Devron's voice was again satirically amused.

'Then, Paul darling, we'll get you to persuade her.'

Both men turned as the silvery voice came from behind them. Valma Kent, in private life Veronica James, had been standing behind them unashamedly listening to their conversation with a fair amount of interest.

'Who could resist the persuasion of Paul Devron?' she added with a mischievous lilt in her voice.

'Plenty,' he answered dryly.

'Did you see that girl ride?' Marriott was more concerned with the rider at the moment than means and methods of persuasion.

'Yes, I saw her.' Valma's voice had changed. Its silvery tones were very soft. 'You could never recapture that scene in a film, Tom. She was alone and obviously thought herself unobserved. Anyway,' she added, with yet another change of tone, 'what makes you think it was your redhead?'

Marriott shrugged. 'Just a hunch. That girl, whoever she was, looked as if she could ride like that.'

'She may not even be able to ride at all,' Devron remarked, with the satirical twitch of one dark brow that had become so well known. 'Your rider in the sunset could be somebody different altogether, fat and cowfaced, or thin and scrawny.'

Valma laughed. 'Give up, Paul. Tom is following one of his hunches. He'll fight tooth and nail to get Miss Unknown Redhead. If she can't ride, well, he'll have her taught.'

Marriott grinned. 'She'll be able to ride,' he said confidently. 'They seem to know her pretty well at those stables.'

Valma reached up and flicked Devron's cheek with slender white fingers.

'And you, my dear Paul, are not quite so indifferent as you like to make out.'

Devron shrugged, but half unconsciously his eyes still searched the hills, as if hoping for another glimpse of the young Diana.

CHAPTER TWO

KERRY slackened her pace as she neared the rambling grey house. It lay in a hollow between low hills. No walls surrounded it, only half wild gardens that gradually merged with and became moorland. An exceedingly small but crystal clear stream wandered through the gardens, delightfully careless of its route. Some miles away it joined a larger stream, which in turn came at last to the deadly Aleyn Bog, where it lost itself.

A tiny bridge crossed the stream a short distance from the house, but Kerry had never bothered to cross it circumspectly and as usual set Smoky over the little stream with effortless ease. On the other side he trotted more sedately towards the weed-grown gravel drive that had once led from well trimmed hedges to The House.

Joddy came out of the stables as she approached. He was in the beginning of his sixties and although his hair was quite white his body was still upright. His hands too were firm and strong as he took Smoky's reins.

'I'll take care of Smoke, Miss Kerry,' he offered, as the girl slid to the ground. 'You don't have much time.'

'Thanks, Joddy,' she answered gratefully, and turned with her graceful yet still boyish stride to the door. There she glanced back. 'Has Rick started getting dressed yet?'

Joddy grinned. 'Yes, Miss Kerry. He wandered in here a little while ago in those full trousers and remarked that it would be more appropriate to go on horseback, instead of by the Squib.'

Kerry, on the move towards the door again, stopped dead. Her green eyes suddenly had an exceedingly speculative and mischievous look. 'That gives me an idea.' Her flaming head went on one side and one bent finger was pressed to her lips. Her eyes were sparkling with a look that became more than just mischievous. She could have been a young Pan, ready to spill out joy of life and eternal glee upon an unsuspecting world. Perhaps not so unsuspecting. Rylston had learned to expect things of an uncommon nature to happen when the Derwins invaded the town for the annual carnival.

Then she sobered and regretfully let the

idea die. 'I guess we'll have to go in the Squib, though. Father seems to think a certain amount of dignity is appropriate on such occasions.'

Joddy blinked innocently. 'Yes, Miss Kerry,' he agreed.

Kerry ran lightly up the three steps to the front door of The House, which as usual stood open, into the wide hall. Its dark wooden floor shone with polish and in one corner stood a huge case that was almost as tall as she was, filled with the feathery fronds of pampas grass. Against one wall stood a small table. Apart from the two items of furniture it was empty, but it did not have a bare look.

A stairway led from the centre of the hallway to the first floor. From a large corridor-landing in the form of a square, ornate metal railings on the side that overlooked the hallway, doors opened into bedrooms. Down below, in the hallway, a long passage along one side of the stairs led straight through to the gardens at the back of the house. The other side was the same, but with a door that led into the space under the stairs, which was used as a storeroom.

Kerry dropped her riding switch on the

low table and opened the door under the stairs. Reaching into the black cavity, she pulled out two swords in ornate metal cases, borrowed from the local antique shop. Holding them carefully, she went up the stairs two at a time and pounded on her brother's door.

The door opened and her twin came out. Except that the fiery mane was cut short there was a remarkable likeness. A short while ago it had been more pronounced, but as both grew older it was diminishing. Rick was now a few inches taller than his sister, a fact that, with the arrogance of eighteen, he did not fail to point out to her with a great deal of satisfaction. In spite of their occasional quarrels, however, there was a very close bond between brother and sister, a unity that had been extended to include dark-haired Kelvin Treveryl. Neither of the boys had ever really treated her as a girl, which perhaps had gone a long way to forming her attitude towards romance in general, although it was a process that had actually been started by her father. Richard Derwin had not quite known what to do with a girl child. He had solved the difficulty very simply, by treating her exactly the same as her brother. Mallie when she had arrived on the scene had been caught in the trap of the flaming Derwin hair and had not been able to bring herself to even try to halt the developing tomboyish tendencies, drowning her conscience with the assurance that the girl would change when she grew up.

So Kerry went to school and behaved more or less like her companions while there, but the moment she was back on the moors she sighed with relief. In the holidays she roamed the moors with her brother and Kelvin Treveryl, until her skin had a perpetual golden tan and her hair seemed to have captured the sunlight in it. She learned to ride almost as soon as she could walk and was sometimes seen mastering a fit of temperament put on by Smoky, laughing, easy in the saddle, with the banner of her hair flying out behind her. The softness of silks and perfumes was not for Kerry Derwin. She laughed and tossed her head at romance and showed no signs of ever wanting to act as other girls.

Her grinning eyes went over her brother, clad in full black trousers and short black boots. The top half of him was covered by a Cossack coat of matching black material, with the typical Russian ornamentation on the front of it.

She looked him up and down and wrinkled her nose in a deliberately insulting grin.

'The Derwins' gift to women. Won't they just love you?'

Rick eyed her darkly. 'You, I take it, are afraid to dress as a girl in case Frank Connors grabs you again,' he retorted.

Kerry shrugged unconcernedly. 'I can handle Frank Connors.' She grinned again and handed over the sword. 'Your sword, Ivan.'

'Thanks.' He clipped it to the black belt around his waist. 'You'd better start getting ready. You'll be late.'

Kerry nodded, her grin dying. 'It doesn't take me long to dress. I'd better eat something first, though, or Mallie will blow a safety valve. I stopped too long looking at Kel's new mare. We're having a picnic tomorrow. He's to . . .' She pulled herself up short. 'Tell you about it later.'

Rick nodded and went inside again, as she turned and ran down the stairs, again two at a time, with perfect balance. This time she was not unobserved and was met at the bottom by a reproachfully tut-tutting

Mallie.

'Miss Kerry! When will you act more ladylike!'

Kerry chuckled and hugged the plump figure. 'Never,' she said unrepentantly, and planted a quick kiss on the rosy cheek, so that the bright blue eyes twinkled in helpless defeat.

'You'll never get married at this rate, child.'

'Heaven forbid!' Kerry retorted quickly. 'Why wish such a fate on me?'

With Mallie following she went into the kitchen and proceeded to eat the food prepared and waiting for her with a speed that brought quite evident but still silent disapproval to the housekeeper's face.

Kerry looked up and grinned. 'Sorry, Mallie, but I'm in a hurry.'

'But what are you going to do if you don't intend to marry?' Mallie went back to the original subject, which was evidently occupying her mind extensively at the moment.

She sounded so worried Kerry stopped eating long enough to contemplate the matter.

Marriage was, of course, quite out of the question. Kisses, light and otherwise, came under the heading of things unpleasant. Since she had never had a proclivity for such things, when the subject crossed her mind at all, her rather nebulous dislike had been crystallized and hardened to a very determined dislike by an unfortunate encounter with Frank Connors.

She could still remember quite well the surprise meeting on one of her lonely picnics. Evidently Connors had been following her. The opportunity had been too good for him to miss. Young Miss Derwin had piqued his vanity by indifference to his complimentary remarks. Young Miss Derwin, far from appreciating his amorous overtures, had also pushed him very violently into the stream by which she had been sitting. She had then vaulted into Smoky's saddle and left the scene in great displeasure.

No, Kerry decided, remembering Connors' podgy hands and the damp mouth she had foiled from touching hers in the nick of time, marriage or even flirtations were definitely not for her.

'I'll have to take up some sort of career,' she decided at last. 'When I mentioned it to Father some time ago he said there was no necessity for it, though.' She glanced at

Mallie and nodded slightly. 'I'll have to tackle him again, really seriously. I'd need to have some sort of training, but the darling idiot seems to think I'll change my mind about getting married.'

'You might, you know,' Mallie pointed out. 'You're growing up and you could change your mind.'

Kerry swallowed a mouthful of tea and shook her head violently. 'That's not likely to happen. Anyway, love is a lot of nonsense.'

Mallie wagged her head wisely. 'It don't do to laugh at love, Miss Kerry. Love always laughs last, you know.'

Kerry finished the tea and laid down the cup. Her green eyes had a hint of teasing. 'Anyway, who do you suggest I marry?'

'Well, there's Kelvin Treveryl...' Mallie began.

Kerry burst into a shout of laughter. 'Oh, heavens! Poor Kel! I must tell him. Anyway,' she added, 'he's too nice to get any silly ideas of that sort.'

'Well, if not him, someone else.' Mallie was not giving up easily. 'It will happen, you mark my words.'

'With big red crosses,' Kerry retorted audaciously. 'X marks the spot—where it never happened!'

Mallie smiled and involuntarily her eyes went over the girl. Some day a man would accept the challenge of those bright green eyes that laughed at love and would kiss those firmly folded but beautiful lips into surrender. She could only hope it was a man worthy of the wonderful creature that was Kerry Derwin.

'You mark my words,' she repeated sententiously. 'There'll be a man one day who won't be put off. Then we'll see who laughs last.'

'Bosh!' retorted Miss Derwin quite inelegantly, as she rose to her feet and crossed to the doorway. 'Thanks for the tea, Mallie.'

When she reached her room, Kerry stripped off her clothes with amazing rapidity and slid into a nearly cold bath. Sometimes the water system at The House was apt to act a little temperamental, but Kerry did not have time to worry much about it at the moment.

She emerged a short time later wrapped in an old blue dressing-gown that clashed horribly with her hair and had been a present from an aunt, now deceased, with no eye for colour. Going to her room, she dressed in a costume that was the counterpart of her brother's. As usual her slimness gave her extra height and her black costume accentuated it. She stamped her feet down into short black boots, the whole ensemble, like her brother's, borrowed from the local dramatic society, and ran a comb through her hair. Then she surveyed herself in some dissatisfaction. Full black tunic swinging, she shot out of the room and, leaning over the rail, looked down into the hallway below and called for Mallie with all the strength of her healthy young lungs.

The housekeeper came from the kitchen regions almost running. 'What's the matter, Miss Kerry?'

Kerry gave her an apologetic grin. 'Sorry to startle you, Mallie. I only wanted to borrow some hairpins.'

'I'll get you some.'

She went back into her room and occupied herself with clipping on the sword, the only thing the dramatic society had not been able to supply. However, old Mr. Johns who owned the antique shop had not been proof against Kerry's persuasion when she caught sight of the swords in the window.

Mallie came into the room with a handful of hairpins, which she tipped on the dressing-table and watched doubtfully as the girl proceeded to scrag her hair up ruthlessly, pinned it securely and then replaced the hat.

The effect was more boyish, but not so startling as when the mane of copper hair had rippled over the black material.

'Oh, your hair!' Mallie lamented.

'It's more in keeping like this,' Kerry answered her very firmly.

There was a peremptory banging on the door that was unmistakably Rick.

'Coming!' Kerry called out, and went to open the door.

Mallie beamed at the pair. She could not help it. They both looked so attractive. Then a heavier tread came down the corridor.

'Let me have a look at you,' Richard Derwin requested, and his son and daughter turned to face him, identical grins on both faces.

'You'll do,' he said simply. 'Enjoy yourselves.' His twinkling eyes went over his daughter. 'And Kerry, please, no . . . er . . . demonstrations of your prowess with the sword.'

Miss Derwin looked unnaturally innocent. 'I can't use a sword,' she said demurely, then the wicked glint was back. 'Unfortunately I haven't a bow and arrow this time.'

'Fortunately or unfortunately is a matter of opinion,' he father retorted dryly. 'And now off with the pair of you.' He leaned over the rail and, spying Joddy in the hall below, very unceremoniously in the usual Derwin manner, called out from his undignified position.

'Have you got the Squib out?'

Joddy looked disconsolate. 'It won't work, sir,' he retorted.

Kerry giggled childishly, 'It's a damp Squib!'

Her father gave her a reproving glance. 'It's not a laughing matter. Now how are you going to get there?'

Rick supplied the answer in one word, as sister and brother looked at each other in carefully hidden delight.

'Ride.'

A shade of indecision crossed the elder Derwin's face and Kerry put in quickly: 'It's the only way, if we're not to be late. We're staying at Kel's place tonight, so the horses can be left there and we can return on them in the morning. Anyway,' she added, 'what could be more appropriate than two Cossacks arriving on horseback?'

Derwin shrugged resignedly, knowing his Cossacks well. 'All right, but promise me one thing, you two,' he added grimly. 'Don't ride those horses up the steps and inside the Hall. Rylston knows we're mad, but keep it more or less stable. Don't make it any worse.'

'Of course,' Kerry promised instantly. Her brother, knowing his sister's versatile imagination, gave his own promise willingly enough. There were other things than actually riding up the steps and into the Hall.

Joddy had already brought the horses around to the front of the house, explaining that as he couldn't get the car going he'd guessed they would have to go that way. Derwin gave him a suspicious glance, but didn't see the wink that only Kerry caught, nor the grin she hastily suppressed. The two redheaded Cossacks then vaulted up into the saddle and were gone.

They knew the path well enough and the night was brightly moonlit. Neck and neck the two horses responded to their riders' urging voices and with the imagination of youth and high spirits the hills of the moors became the faraway plains of the steppes.

But there was one thing wrong. Kerry was not used to having her hair confined. Pins were sticking into her from every direction. One impatient hand went up and ripped off her hat. Within seconds the wind had done its work and Mallie's hairpins were scattered over the moors. Tucking the reins under one knee and without slackening her pace, Kerry raised both hands to set the hat back on her head and adjust it.

During the ride brother and sister spoke little. It was difficult when the wind blew away their words and time would not allow them to slacken their pace. They didn't want to. The thrill of the thundering hooves and powerful muscles beneath them was racing in their veins.

When they arrived at the Treveryl household, Kelvin was waiting for them. At his surprised look, seeing they were riding, Kerry leaned down from her saddle and spoke quickly. For a moment he looked startled, then chuckled softly. Without hesitation he turned and a short while later came out leading the golden mare.

Rylston, gay already with the spirit of carnival, was suddenly startled to hear the thunder of hooves in the direction of the far end of the main street. The small party that had just left a car outside the Hall where the carnival was being held turned to follow the wondering looks of the people around them.

Colonel Treveryl was the first to guess what was happening. 'The Cossacks!' His voice was half startled, widely expectant.

'The Cossacks?' The tall, black-haired man at his side repeated the words in an interrogatory tone.

'My son and the two Derwins,' Treveryl explained. 'I had half a suspicion that they'd be up to something this year as well.'

The thunder of hooves was coming closer now. The Mayor of Rylston, one of the party, hastily covered a smile.

'A most regrettable incident last year,' he mumbled.

'What happened?'

It was the black-haired man who again spoke and Colonel Treveryl glanced at him with a smile.

'Kerry Derwin went as Robin Hood. She accidentally shot an arrow into the headgear of a dignified dowager. Somehow

I have an idea that our Kerry's aim was just a little too good. She'd been very assiduously practising for quite a while before.'

A faint, enigmatic smile played around Paul Devron's firm lips. There was something intriguing about this Kerry Derwin, especially if she was the rider of the sunset.

The thunder of hooves was almost on them now and then the three horses swept around the corner and a gasp came from the onlookers. All three riders were standing in their saddles, hand on hips, with perfect balance. As they went by Kerry caught a glimpse of the group who had been about to enter the Hall.

Colonel Treveryl and the Mayor were familiar figures. She recognized also the short, wiry man she had previously seen talking to the Colonel. The remaining two members of the party were equally familiar. Valma Kent, with her silver-fair hair and large grey eyes and the slender, beautiful figure that was clothed in sophisticated black. There was a smile of appreciation on the lovely features and the grey eyes were interested and frankly amused.

The man at her side, in formal evening

dress, also needed no introduction. His dark attraction was a perfect foil for her fairness. The lights outside the Hall shone on raven black hair and eyes that were no shade lighter watched the riders intently. He had the darkness of the Latin, but his tall slenderness and sharp features were not theirs. Officially Paul Devron was French-Canadian.

Then the riders were past, although not yet out of sight—and Kerry's hat blew off. Her hair, merely piled up beneath the hat without the pins, streamed down gloriously free.

Without hesitation, she dropped expertly back into the saddle and wheeled Smoky. For a moment the vicious-looking stallion reared, pawing the air and bringing a gasp from the onlookers, then he was again nearing the group at the doorway, who were slowly recovering from their paralysis.

A black astrakhan hat landed almost at Paul Devron's feet and as he bent to pick it up a grey stallion suddenly reared in front of him. A slim, black-clothed figure leaned from the saddle and snatched it up almost from beneath his fingers.

As she wheeled yet again, controlling the excitedly rearing Smoky, Kerry had a glimpse of dark eyes from which the cynical boredom had entirely gone. They challenged her with amused speculation and unconsciously her upflung head accepted the challenge, then she was gone, had caught up with Rick and Kelvin, who had slowed to await her further on.

Tom Marriott blinked. He looked bemused. 'Who was she?'

'Kerry Derwin,' Treveryl said succinctly.

Marriott began to come out of his daze. His eyes snapped. 'That's the girl!' he said excitedly.

'The young Diana.' Paul Devron's voice was soft, the famous voice with its faint, almost unnoticeable accent, that had stirred the susceptible hearts of so many women.

'Interested?' Valma whispered at his side.

His expression became indifferent. 'In a redheaded child?' He shrugged and turned aside to follow the rest of the party in.

The three Cossacks meantime had circled round to the back of the town and regained the Treveryl stables. They left the horses in the hands of grinning and sympathetic grooms and began to walk to the Hall.

Kerry spent some moments trying to bundle her rebellious hair back under the hat, but it was impossible.

'Leave it.' Kelvin gave the flaming red mane an idle glance. He was used to it. 'That mop will probably push it off anyway if you try to stuff it inside the hat.' A teasing glint entered his eyes. 'I'm surprised at you, though, throwing your hat at Paul Devron's feet!'

Kerry stopped dead in her indignation. 'I didn't,' she denied hotly. 'The wretched thing blew off.'

Rick winked at Kelvin. 'I was beginning to suspect that she was just as bad as the rest of them. She rushed off to see one of his films this afternoon.'

'I didn't!' Nothing annoyed Kerry more than to be accused of romantic motivations. It only added insult to injury that this time it was Paul Devron. She began to get furious and as usual coherency departed from her speech. 'At least, I mean I saw the film, but I was forced . . . I mean Barbie dragged me off. The idiot had to see it the moment it came on and her mother wouldn't let her go alone.' She snorted with youthful scorn. 'She probably knew Barbie would come out in a daze. I had to darn near slap her to get her out of it.'

They were still wrangling good-naturedly when they reached the Hall and there they were pounced on by a crowd of their friends. Barbie, masquerading as a Spanish girl, left her parents to join them. Every now and again her eyes ranged the Hall, as if seeking someone. The three knew who she was looking for and grinned at each other without comment. Then Kerry gave a groan as she saw a tall, blonde girl in a Grecian costume approaching them.

'Quick, Kel,' she whispered urgently. 'Dance with me. I think I'm about to get a lecture from Merle!'

'O.K.,' Kelvin said good-humouredly, and put his arm around her to start dancing.

It was a waltz and, although he danced well, Kerry for the moment didn't have her mind on dancing. A little curiously she analysed just what sort of feeling having his arm around her gave her, blaming the unusual track of her thoughts on Mallie's words. No effect at all so far as she could see. Everything was perfectly normal. She dismissed with a shrug of mental ridicule the idea that it could ever be anything else.

Such things could not affect her.

That matter settled quite satisfactorily, she gave herself up to the pleasure dancing always gave her. There was a pleasure she could understand in fitting rhythmic steps to gay music. Kelvin was a good dancer and she liked dancing with him more than anyone else. He didn't try to hold her closer than the dance permitted, as some of her other partners occasionally did—to be speedily disillusioned of the idea that their efforts were appreciated. Anyway, it was ridiculous to think of Kelvin trying anything like that; Kel, whom she had known for years.

Kerry, as usual, was blithely oblivious of anything different and thoroughly enjoyed the dance. Both Rick and herself were exceptionally good dancers too. Their mother had given her exquisite grace to both her children. Rick had the suppleness of the dancer in his movements, while with Kerry it was a living flame.

As the music stopped and they walked to the edge of the floor, Kerry heard a voice behind her.

'Kerry, I want to speak to you.'

She gave a silent groan and turned slowly. 'Oh, hallo, Merle.' Her expression was carefully blank. 'What about?'

The older girl made a quick, exasperated gesture. She was lovely in a cold fashion-plate way and beautifully made up. Her gown was expensive and obviously created by a master hand, but the expression in her too light blue eyes was hard.

'My dear child, surely you don't need to be told.' Her tone had a faintly supercilious contempt, which was reflected in her eyes as they rested on Kerry. 'Your conduct tonight was deplorable.'

'In what way?' Kerry's voice was quiet. Inside she was conscious of a surge of very active dislike that could burst into flame at much more provocation.

'Throwing yourself at Paul Devron like that.' Merle's light eyes were cold and furious and she ignored the danger signals beginning to show in Kerry's face. 'After all, Rylston does have a reputation to keep up and yours is one of the leading families, although you seem to forget it too often.'

Kerry felt the hot colour rising to her face and her eyes sparkled dangerously. Kelvin's warning grip on her arm tightened.

'Come and dance,' he said calmly, and swung her on to the floor again.

Merle Connors stood there a moment, her face made quite unattractive for a brief instant by the flash of hatred that crossed it. At times Kerry wondered at the intensity of Merle's dislike of her, as she had never done anything to hurt Merle. It was just that always when they met something antagonistic flared between them.

Merle turned with an impatient gesture to climb the stairs that led to a balcony set with chairs and tables and occupied at one end by a refreshment bar. The largest table was presided over by her mother, a wealthy widow with the snobbishness of the social climber. There were five empty seats. Tom Marriott, Valma Kent and Paul Devron and her own partner, a fair nonentity of a man, occupied the remaining seats.

Merle slid into one of the empty seats and smiled at the actor. 'I must apologize for Kerry Derwin's conduct, Mr. Devron. I'm afraid that little show was staged just with the intention of gaining your attention.'

Devron gave a small, enigmatic smile, but Marriott shrugged carelessly.

'Oh, Paul is used to women throwing themselves at him.'

The music had stopped and, by some unfortunate coincidence, Kerry and Kelvin had left the floor directly below the balcony where the film party were sitting. The voices of both Merle and Tom Marriott drifted down quite audibly.

The sardonic amusement in Devron's eyes deepened. 'Thanks for the warning,' he said dryly, 'but cradle-snatching is not one of my vices.'

Merle flushed and for a moment a strained silence reigned over the table. Hastily Valma tried to change the subject.

'This is a very modern club you have,' she remarked, a little too quickly, and very gladly Merle plunged off on to the new track, until out of the corner of her eyes she caught someone trying to attract her attention and relievedly excused herself.

Valma leaned across and tapped Paul lightly on the arm.

'You shouldn't have said that, Paul. Everybody knows the reputation you have where women are concerned.'

His eyes narrowed savagely. 'My reputation! Whose fault is that? Can I help it if women will make fools of themselves—' He broke off and smiled apologetically, his dark eyes glinting. 'Did I sound conceited?

I'm sorry. But when people start giving me warnings . . .'

He fell silent, his dark eyes morose now. He knew he had some peculiar and very potent fascination for women, it was inevitable that he should know, but except on the screen, where it was his work, he had never used it deliberately. Of the many women who had offered him their love, only few had known the invitation accepted. He would not have been human if there hadn't been such instances, but even so the most dangerous game of all was only played with those who understood and accepted its rules. Warm blood ran in his veins, but he had never once taken advantage of the subtle magnetism given to him by the mixing of the cool blood of England and the quicker blood of France.

Valma leaned across and again touched his arm, but this time it was consolingly.

'Forget it, Paul. She didn't mean anything by it.'

His mouth twisted in a faintly ironic smile. 'Perhaps not, but I hardly looked at the girl.'

Valma laughed. 'Don't get so heated,' she said calmly. 'Everyone knows it's not your fault that women fall for you.' Her eyes twinkled. 'Even though one of your fans did climb through your bedroom window one night,' she added wickedly.

A flush rose up under his dark tan. 'Don't bring that up, please.' He laughed as he looked at her smiling face and the storm died out of his eyes. 'You know, Valma, if you weren't already married, I think I would have annexed you myself.'

'Then perhaps it's just as well,' she retorted. 'I would hate to have to chase ardent fans out of the house on my honeymoon!'

Something brought Valma's head up to look behind him. There she met a pair of green eyes that were brilliant with barely restrained fury. An expression of dismay crossed her face. The girl wore the costume of a Cossack and a mane of red hair hung to her shoulders. There was no doubt at all who it was.

It was unfortunate that Kerry had been standing where she could hardly help but overhear the conversation of the film stars. Already flaming over Merle's remarks, she was now quite speechless. For a moment she seemed unable to move. Anger had paralysed her very limbs. Wild ideas rioted in her mind. She would go up to Paul

Devron and in very decided terms assure him that she had no desire to speak to him either. Her fingers itched to strike that dark cheek, but still she did not move. She had not known she was capable of such intense and concentrated hatred.

She saw Valma's hand move slightly and Devron's head begin to turn at the expression on his companion's face, then she turned and ran, choking back the sob of sheer fury that rose to her lips. Even when she reached the other three in the refreshment room, her eyes were still glowing with the aftermath of her anger and Kelvin glanced at her curiously.

'What's the matter? Run into Frank Connors again?'

'No!' She almost spat the word out. Controlling her still considerable rage with difficulty, she jerked out a few short sentences of explanation.

Rick grinned. 'Don't take any notice of it. All film stars are conceited.'

Kerry scowled and attacked an ice-cream with concentrated venom. It was quite evident that she wished it was someone else she was attacking and with something more deadly than a spoon.

How dared he! The insufferable conceit

of the man! As if she had any desire at all to even see him, let alone speak to him. The fact that so many stupid women had made fools of themselves over him and many more had written him letters dripping with sentimental tripe had probably made him imagine that every woman he came in contact with was in love with him.

She scooped up the last of the ice-cream with a ferocity that made the metal of the spoon screech against the china and Kelvin gave her an amused look.

'Don't break the plate! That's not Devron.'

Kerry thumped the plate down on the table and gradually the lingering remnants of her scowl died away in a grin. Luckily her rages were always short-lived, but they were intense while they lasted.

'The ice-cream's cooled her down,' Rick commented as they went out on the balcony.

Out of the corner of her eye Kerry noticed that the two film stars were no longer there and felt much happier. The sight of Paul Devron near at hand would probably have sent her fury soaring again.

'It must be about time for the judging of the costumes,' Barbie remarked.

Kelvin nodded and glanced over the balcony. The ball had not long been in progress, but the judging was to be early, to give the two stars the chance to leave if they desired to do so.

There was a fanfare from the band and Paul Devron and Valma Kent walked out on to the stage, to the accompaniment of loud clapping. There was a ripple of excitement evident over the whole of the hall.

Barbie sidled nearer to Kerry and whispered: 'He's just as good-looking as he is on the screen.'

Kerry didn't say a word.

'I wonder what this mysterious raffle is that Merle seems to have arranged,' Barbie went on. 'She said . . .'

'If you keep quiet you'll hear,' Kerry put in. 'They're announcing it now.'

The Mayor had held up his hand for silence. It was only a short announcement, but it brought a rousing cheer from the audience.

Kerry wrinkled her nose in disgust. 'Trust Merle Connors to think of something like that!'

Her brother looked at her consideringly, his head on one side. 'Wouldn't you like to win a kiss from Paul Devron?'

Kerry gave him a withering glance.

'I'd like to win it,' Barbie announced brightly, and they all laughed.

'I don't think I'll bother to go down for the judging,' Kerry decided. 'Our three costumes are the same, not that they're in the least original in any case.'

'I'd like to go down,' Barbie said, and glanced at Rick.

'All right,' he agreed, good-naturedly, and looked over towards Kelvin. 'Are you coming down, or staying here with Kerry?'

Kelvin nodded. 'I'll stay here.'

Watching from the balcony they saw the other two come out below and join the procession for the judging. Immediately after the prizes had been given it was decided to draw the raffle. Both of them burst out laughing when one of the shyest boys in the neighbourhood won the raffle, but nevertheless went up quite determinedly to collect his prize—a kiss from Valma Kent.

Then the Mayor's hand was dipping into the bowl that held the women's tickets.

'Number seventy-four!'

'I wonder who the unfortunate girl is,' Kerry commented, and sniffed inelegantly.

There seemed to be some delay. The girl with ticket number seventy-four didn't appear to claim her prize. People were beginning to look around them.

'The idiot's probably swooned with delight,' Kerry went on caustically.

'What number do you have?' Kelvin asked.

Kerry shrugged and dug around for her ticket, then an expression of acute dismay crossed her face. It was impossible!

'Number seventy-four,' she said weakly.

It couldn't be true! But it was. There was 74 very plainly on the ticket. To think that she had won such an unwelcome and unwanted prize! A kiss from Paul Devron. She could just imagine herself going down there and submitting like some simpering fool. Her red hair bristled at the very thought.

Kelvin almost choked. 'This is going to be good!'

Good! That wasn't the word. Kerry eyed him darkly and had plans regarding the immediate destruction of ticket number seventy-four.

'Oh no, it isn't,' she retorted. 'They can make another draw. I'm staying right here,' She very determinedly ripped up the ticket until there was no chance of identifying the number and nodded with great satisfaction. 'Now they won't know who had ticket number seventy-four.'

'Oh yes, they will,' he sent back delightedly. 'There was a note taken of every ticket sold and who had it. After the fun you had with your hat everybody knows you arrived all right. You'll just have to face the music. I'll stand by with a pick-me-up,' he offered, grinning.

'You won't.' Her stubborn chin had set. The thought of going downstairs was unthinkable. To her kisses never were a pleasant prospect and after the remarks she had overheard Paul Devron's variety were more than unwelcome. 'You can go down there and tell them to try again. Tell them I went home or . . . or something.'

Kelvin's grin grew taunting. 'Go down and tell them yourself—or are you frightened he might grab you?'

'Certainly not,' she flashed back.

'All right,' he agreed instantly. 'I'll go down.'

Kerry smiled in relief. 'Thanks, Kel. I'll jump the barrier and go up to the second balcony. I'll be out of sight altogether there.'

They went back to the stairway, but when he turned to go downstairs she vaulted over a low barrier on the upward stairway to the disused second balcony. Within seconds she was out of sight and nobody on the almost deserted first balcony had seen her go.

On the stage the Mayor was consulting a list. He swallowed hard when he saw the name against number seventy-four and showed it to the master of ceremonies. The latter stepped forward to the microphone.

'Will Miss Kerry Derwin please come to the stage?' Turning, he muttered an aside to the Mayor, unaware that Devron heard him. 'Ten to one our readhead wildcat is missing. You know what usually happens when anybody tries to kiss her. Frank Connors landed in the brook!'

An impish smile came into Valma's lovely eyes. 'Want to bet she's missing?' she whispered.

Paul smiled. 'What happens to my vanity and reputation?'

And then in the hushed expectancy that had held the dancers since the announcement of the name, a figure was seen approaching through the crowd. It was in Cossack dress, but it was brown-haired.

'It's Kelvin,' the Mayor said softly.

Kelvin walked leisurely and unconcernedly towards the stage and looked up at the Mayor.

'I think you'd better try again.' He paused and then added: 'The heat made her feel a bit faint and she went out for some air.'

A low murmur of subdued laughter ran through the hall. They knew it was only a subterfuge. If young Kerry had felt faint at all it was because of the discovery of her ticket number.

Before the Mayor could speak, Devron stepped to the edge of the stage. 'I'm sorry to hear that,' he said with perfect composure. 'Offer Miss Derwin my apologies and tell her that I'll pay my debt at some other time.'

For a moment Kelvin's eyes narrowed in warning and blue eyes looked into black, then he nodded.

'I'll tell her.' As he turned away, he added a parting shot. 'By the way, I hope you're insured. She doesn't like being kissed.'

By the time he reached Rick and Barbie the two stars had left the stage and had disappeared. Kerry was still missing.

Kerry reached the balcony and leaned against the rail, her panic slowly subsiding. She didn't think Paul Devron had seen her come upstairs and even if he had, he wasn't likely to suspect the second darkened and railed-off stairway, even if he had tried to follow her, which seemed an unlikely action on his part. She felt a faint, mischievous triumph at outwitting him.

She laughed softly—and then froze. While she had been enjoying her triumph the object of her thoughts had crossed on silent footsteps to stand at her side. Leaning on the balcony, he looked down at her. She straightened up and instinctively backed a few steps. One hand went out, as if to ward him off.

'You needn't run.' The soft musical voice with its faint trace of accent was only too familiar. 'I'm not going to kiss you.'

His words had the effect of stiffening her into belligerency. 'You'd better not try it!'

'No?' There was lazy amusement in his tone. 'Why not?'

Kerry blinked and for the moment all ideas of flight went out of her head. She wasn't used to being questioned on that particular subject. Usually she was taken at her word. If not, she took measures to prove her point. Now that she came to think of it, though, she was not at all sure what her objections were.

He straightened up off the balcony and instantly suspicious she tensed, but he laughed and shook his head.

'You're still quite safe.'

Once again, when every instinct urged her to fly, she hesitated, surprised to see that he was smiling and that one hand was held out to her

'You overheard something I said earlier. I didn't mean it. Will you forgive me?'

Kerry's lips parted in startled surprise at his words. This didn't have the sound of conceit.

The old stubborn Kerry, reluctant to revise her opinion of him, wanted to throw his apology in his face, to say that what he said or thought didn't bother her, but to her surprise she saw her hand go out to meet his with a volition of its own and gave it a look of disbelief, as if it had detached itself from the rest of her body and turned traitor.

The strong fingers closed round hers warmly and sent a strange little tingling feeling through her, so that she tugged her hand free, thrusting it boyishly into a pocket of her costume.

'Why did you say it?' Kerry spoke quickly, to hide the confusion the tingling in her fingers had given her.

He shrugged. 'I was angry, someone had just said something that annoyed me, then your name was mentioned and I'm afraid you bore the brunt of it.' He smiled whimsically. 'Don't you ever say things when you're angry that you regret afterwards?'

A reluctant smile tugged at the corner of her mouth. 'Quite often,' she admitted in fellow feeling. Her eyes lowered. 'My hat really did come off by accident. I didn't do it deliberately to attract your attention.'

A peremptory finger beneath her chin tipped her head up and made her meet his eyes. They were serious now and faintly frowning.

'What gave you that impression?'

Her eyes fell from his. Somehow she couldn't meet their intense darkness, although there was nothing personal about them now. Also, strangely, his touching her didn't make her flare up.

'Well, Mer . . .' She had been going to say that Merle had warned her of the possible construction of her action, but stopped. Much as she disliked Merle Connors, her code wouldn't allow her to repeat what had been said to her. 'Just something I overheard,' she finished instead.

'Then whatever it was and whoever said it was a very stupid person,' he said very firmly, and she had an insane desire to giggle. 'Far from gaining that impression,' he added, and her serious expression lightened, 'I wondered for the moment whether you intended to hit me in the face with that hat, or merely trample me underfoot.'

Her gamin smile flashed out. 'Smoky was rather excited.'

'With reason,' he agreed dryly. 'That was quite a show you put on. Where did you learn to ride like that?'

She shrugged carelessly. She didn't think of her riding as anything so special.

'From the Colonel.'

He turned slightly, so that he could look down into the vivid face. Kerry looked back at him quite without embarrassment. There was something in his regard strangely reassuring, yet not altogether impersonal now. Even though she was unconscious of it, the subtle magnetism of the man was already affecting her. It was in his voice, in the tall arrogance of him outlined so clearly in the light coming up from below, the dark aquiline features that had nothing of the insipidness of the matinee idol and the black eyes dancing with amusement at her intent regard.

She had a sudden vision of him in the film she had seen him in that afternoon. He had taken the part of an outlaw capturing his bride by force. The strong brown hands had been ruthless, but his voice and eyes dangerously caressing. He had kissed his reluctant bride (who was greatly to be pitied, of course) with a blend of that same ruthlessness and a demanding ardour that was equally effective.

Kerry had expected him to be the same off the screen, conceited and very sure of his attraction, although why she should have thought that it was hard to explain. He didn't even give that impression on the screen.

But he was different altogether. He was likeable. Reluctantly she admitted it to herself, and then not so reluctantly.

'Mr Devron . . .' she began.

'Paul,' he corrected. He bent down.

'What is it?'

'Oh... Oh, nothing,' she said undecidedly. 'It's just that you're... Well, you're different from what I imagined.'

He laughed outright at that and Kerry found she didn't mind him laughing at her.

'Off the screen, in spite of my reputation, I don't go around abducting helpless maidens—and I should be exceedingly wary of those who rode grey stallions Cossack fashion.' He paused and added a little quizzically, 'I wonder what you would have done, young lady, if you'd been down in the hall when that raffle was drawn just now.'

Kerry grinned impudently. 'More to the point, what would you have done?'

He appeared to give the matter thoughtful consideration. 'That's rather hard to answer, since you weren't in the hall, unfortunately.' As he added the last word, the laughter was back in his voice.

'Fortunately,' Kerry countered instantly.

'That's a matter of opinion,' he stated with great firmness. He took her hand and tucked it through his arm. 'Do you think Miss Derwin would dance with me if I asked her nicely?'

'Miss Derwin doesn't seem to have much choice,' she retorted, finding herself being led towards the stairway.

'Don't answer back,' he warned. 'You might make me regret my decision not to pay my debt, not at the moment anyway.'

'You'd better not try it at any time,' Kerry informed him pugnaciously.

He put on a mock injured air. 'Young lady, I'm told I do it rather well.'

In spite of the nature of his joking words, she found her liking for him increasing and it showed in her expressive face. More strange, she actually found herself wondering what it would be like to be kissed by him. Involuntarily, she flashed him a quick, upward glance, hoping she was unobserved, which she was not. He seemed to notice her every action and glance.

It wouldn't be like being kissed by Frank Connors, who hadn't succeeded anyway in his aim. Paul's kiss wouldn't be damp and flabby, as she had sensed Connors' would have been. His lips were well formed, although a trifle sensuous, and somehow she knew their touch would be pleasant and perhaps even exciting. Then, startled at the unusual and revolutionary trend of her truant thoughts, she hastily thrust them from her.

They reached the top of the stairs and Kerry began to pick her way carefully downwards, acutely conscious of Paul's nearness and the arm upon which her hand rested. It was so different for her to be aware of anybody as a man and herself as a girl that she couldn't fight it, not yet anyway. She could only let it sweep over her and enjoy the sensation. She even admitted it to herself. It was enjoyable.

She was so occupied with her thoughts that she missed a step and but for the quick arm that went around her would have fallen.

'Careful,' Paul's voice said above her head.

Delicious bubbling laughter welled up inside her. 'What of—the stairs or you?'

The arm around her waist tightened, drawing her back hard against him. 'You little devil,' he said softly.

Kerry, becoming alarmed, discovered she had been playing with fire. His hand came up to her throat, pressing her head back against his shoulder with a strength she knew she had no hope of fighting. His head was bent, very near to hers. His eyes were on her lips with such meaning that she found herself trembling.

'If you make challenging remarks like that, you'll have to learn to accept the consequences.' His voice was husky and his faint accent seemed more noticeable.

Kerry discovered that her heart was pounding as it never had before and that all strength seemed to have gone from her limbs, leaving her limp and helpless in his hold. She couldn't understand why she was so totally unable to fight. Usually she was full of fury.

His lips were so near to hers she could feel his warm breath on her face and involuntarily she closed her eyes, surrendering to the inevitable—and then she was released, swaying slightly and unconsciously gripping his arm for support.

'It would have served you right if I had kissed you.' His voice was firm and the arm she gripped hard with tension.

Kerry swallowed hard and looked up at him, then as quickly her glance fell. Illogically she found she was disappointed and there was a chill feeling where the warmth of his hand had rested on her neck.

When they reached the bottom of the stairway, instead of letting her jump over on her own, he put both hands on either side of her waist and lifted her over with easy strength, then vaulted over lightly himself. Kerry stood there with her breath again coming unusually fast.

At the foot of the second flight of stairs, he drew her into his arms and began dancing. Again she was conscious of being so close to him, as she had never been while dancing with anyone else. The music and rhythm seemed to have an entirely different meaning. Because she was dancing with Paul Devron.

CHAPTER THREE

In spite of the late hour she had gone to bed, Kerry awoke early. The grey light of dawn was only just stealing through the window of her room at the Treveryl home, and a glance at her watch confirmed the suspicion that her thoughts had been too confused to even let her sleep.

She sat up slowly, thrusting the tumbled hair back off her face with a worried gesture. Her eyes were frowning with the knowledge that last night she hadn't been acting quite the same as usual. It was hard to define the actual difference. Or was it? The cause and the effect led only to one person—Paul Devron. Was she about to make as big a fool of herself as all the others?

It was an unpalatable and decidedly unacceptable thought. Swiftly, she swung out of bed, as if action would thrust it from her.

In spite of the severely tailored pyjamas, there was nothing boyish about her as she stood at the window. Her slender body had the alert tension of the quarry that for the first time scents the hunter on its trail and, with complete certainty, she knew that she wouldn't have felt or even acknowledged the warning but for the lingering remnants of the new femininity that had awakened in her last night. The old Kerry Derwin would have had nothing of it.

Slowly she turned, leaning against the wall. Very little of importance had happened after they had come down from the balcony. Paul had danced with her and then had disappeared to talk to Valma, leaving Kerry with a curious sense of loss.

Then a peculiarly suspicious Kelvin had taken her off to dance. With an obstinate awkwardness she had been deliberately evasive and came near to precipitating what was the first real quarrel she had ever had with him.

Dancing with Paul had made her sink deeper into the strange mesh of enchantment she had felt during their talk on the balcony. The impact of his virile and arrogant personality, the dark attraction of him, had been too much for her total inexperience to withstand.

But this was morning. The old Kerry Derwin was not dead and she didn't like the idea at all of the new Kerry Derwin who had been dominant last night.

She straightened off the wall with a scowl and a sound that was like a grunt. A lock of flaming hair flopped forward over her forehead and her shoulders hunched. Her arms folded across her chest and she regarded her reflection, seen in the mirror across the room, with acute dislike.

'Idiot!' she addressed it, and it scowled back at her.

She stalked across the room and glared at the reflection. Somehow it seemed to her to be not her own, but the Kerry Derwin's of the night before. As such it deserved her present scorn and contempt. It had been a so gullible and easily tricked reflection.

Virile and arrogant! The dark attraction of him! The two Kerry Derwins scowled at each other. Facile, artificial charm, one of them snapped. She moved and the reflection was gone from the mirror. The Kerry Derwin of last night had disappeared.

This was morning and the vagaries of last night were destroyed. Of course it had been his vanity that had been wounded, she decided scornfully. He wasn't used to his kisses being refused. It had been that which had made him return and seek her out. But even so, with the excuse of last night not seeing through to the damaged and revenge-seeking male ego, and believing his interest real, she had still not explained her own feelings. They could not be satisfactorily explained in the light of cold reason—without dangerous admissions at least. Those she did not want to make. She didn't even intend to contemplate them.

With a very un-Kerryish dishonesty, she promptly buried her head in comforting and blanketing mental sand and pretended they had never existed. In a panic she banished the awakening femininity that might have grown, to show her the trap beneath her feet.

It was easy to rouse anger now when she thought of the episode on the stairs, instead of the breathless pleasure it had really given her. The arm around her waist had not evoked a thrill of excitement; it had been a helpless fury at the strength that had held her. That breathless thrill had been nausea and the warmth of his hand on her neck had been frighteningly hot. How dared he maul her about?

She added that final insult and felt much better. She even managed a satisfied smile. Miss Derwin had explained her actions and feelings to her complete satisfaction at last—but perhaps not to that of Kerry Derwin of last night, the Kerry Derwin who was being firmly sat on, squashed, derided and almost argued out of existence.

That somewhat difficult task accomplished, she returned to bed and lay there with her arms behind her head, thinking of the day in front of her and refusing to let her mind go backwards, which it had a regrettable tendency to do, in spite of the firmest control. What she wouldn't admit, of course, was that nothing about last night had been in the least controllable.

Slowly the morning grew later. The sun came higher and poured its rays through the window. Somewhere a bird twittered shrilly and its mate answered. For a moment there was silence, then the two came together, a sweet fluting that was spring and youth and love.

Miss Derwin didn't think so. She scowled blackly again and thumped her pillow. Her rolling efforts to snatch a further short sleep, to make up for what her chaotic thoughts had deprived her of, were completely fruitless. Rolled up in the tangled blankets she looked like a peculiar, flame-topped cocoon. Finally she rolled over on her back again, giving up the idea of ever sleeping throughout the rest of her life, and regarded the ceiling with a particularly jaundiced eye. The birds were still singing outside. In fact the whole world was occupied with love, she decided sulkily. She was young and spring was awakening in her veins. Deny its existence as she might, she was no longer the same Kerry Derwin as she had been yesterday morning. Then she had not met an arrogant dark-haired man whose eyes were impudently amused and challenging.

Oh, drat the man! Why wouldn't he stay out of her thoughts? Did he have to intrude his annoying presence at every opportunity?

Scowling yet again, she thrust small, neat feet to the ground and jerked herself stiffly upright. Quickly she bathed and as quickly dressed. Swift action seemed to be the only antidote. She did feel somewhat more settled when dressed in the Cossack costume, all that she had to wear, but her attitude was still just a little truculent and even belligerent.

Before going down she crossed to the window again. This time Kelvin was below, talking to one of the grooms. They finished their conversation and the groom left. For a moment Kelvin still remained standing there. He looked somehow older. Last night he had been boyish. This morning he was a man—even Kerry's undiscerning eye saw that. Last night had been a night of many changes and discoveries.

As if some sixth sense had warned of her watching eyes, Kelvin looked up and their eyes met. And that too was different. For a moment his had something bright and bitter and then an inscrutability yesterday's Kelvin Treveryl could never have possessed.

'Good morning,' he called up to her. 'Rick is already at breakfast.'

She replied to his greeting and added: 'He's started early.'

A brief flicker of a smile crossed his face. 'We were to go on a picnic this morning, remember.' A shadow erased the smile, a shadow that was only half concealed of worry and doubt. 'That's if you still want to go.'

Kerry stiffened. She knew what he meant, but chose to pretend ignorance of something she wouldn't admit.

'What do you mean? Of course I still want to go. Why shouldn't I?'

The inscrutability of his expression broke momentarily, but the expression that took its place was still something she couldn't read.

'That's not something we can discuss at the moment,' he said quietly.

At the moment! That implied the threat of future discussion. And she didn't want to exhume the happenings of last night. A childish annoyance with Kelvin as the innocent cause of allowing her mind to slip the rein of control and remind her of last night, of the unusual pleasure of being held in a man's arms, sent a mutinous twist to her lips. She gripped the windowsill with stiff fingers, leaning forward slightly and in a mood to flare up if any further reference was passed to what she had decided was best forgotten.

Perhaps Kelvin recognized the danger signals. He gave an apparently careless shrug and gestured towards the door.

'Come and eat.'

When Kerry reached the breakfast room only Kelvin and her brother were in possession of it. Luckily in view of what came later, Colonel Treveryl had breakfasted earlier and departed.

Rick ran a critical eye over his sister as she entered. 'Huh!' he remarked, in a tone calculated to draw forth comment. 'You look more yourself this morning.'

Kelvin tried to catch Rick's eye as Kerry's head came up with a jerk, but the boy was too intent on the golden opportunity of having a real opportunity to bait his sister on a subject that was always guaranteed to rouse her.

Her chin was already squaring belligerently. 'What do you mean?'

Kelvin looked from one to the other of them, expecting an explosion any moment, but powerless to stop it. He had half expected a little of the usual brother's blunt tactlessness towards his sister from Rick, but had decided against a warning, since, in spite of their unity, the twins seemed to take a fiendish delight in teasing each other. Usually both could take as well as give, but he knew instinctively that this was something Kerry couldn't be teased about.

Rick was not so sensitive. He leaned his elbows on the table and regarded his sister with a youthful mocking eye.

'What do I mean?' he jeered. 'Talk about the mighty falling! You hit the ground with a loud thump last night. You were as moony-eyed over him as everyone else.'

Kerry turned a brick red, but realized somewhere at the back of her mind that to give too much point to the matter would lead Rick to the belief that he really was on the track of something, which of course he wasn't, another part of her mind put in quickly. She attempted to clamp down, rather unsuccessfully on her rising temper.

'Over who?' she snapped, with scant regard for grammar.

'Who do you think?' Rick sent back gleefully.

Kerry's restraint snapped. Her temper was too much for the temporary rein put on it.

'I'm fed up with your silly, childish teasing!' she flared, and rising to her feet ran out of the room, leaving her breakfast untouched.

This was such an unprecedented happening, Kerry was usually healthily ravenous in the morning, that it completely silenced Rick. His open-mouthed consternation would have been comical in other circumstances, but this was serious. When Rick's mouth closed slowly and it looked as if he was about to speak, Kelvin cut in quickly.

'Keep off the subject of Devron, at least for a while.' While Rick was still looking flabbergasted, he rose to his feet and followed Kerry out.

He found Kerry on the other side of the gate that led out into the paddock. She was sitting on the grass, unheeding whether or not damage came to the costume. That was not like her. She was usually very careful of property not her own. Her head was propped in her hands and that too was unlike her. When she saw him approaching, she jumped quickly to her feet, an instinctive wariness in her eyes and a sense of reluctant shame in her heart. She knew she had acted badly, but knowing and admitting it didn't make her feel any better. She was too mixed up and confused, in spite of the intensive and severe talking-to she had given herself earlier in the morning.

There was a wariness in her eyes that had never been there with Kelvin before. Involuntarily he put out a hand, as if he tried to stop her fleeing from him. Then he smiled at her.

'You don't have to be on guard with me, Kerry. Surely you know that.'

He watched her with grave, thoughtful eyes and Kerry managed a rueful smile.

'Yes, I know that,' she admitted in a low voice. 'I'm sorry, Kel. I didn't mean to flare up like that. It's . . . it's just that Rick caught me on the raw. Usually I can take teasing, you know that, but I just can't stand Paul Devron.'

Kelvin's mouth twitched grimly. He had his own ideas on that subject, but he kept them to himself.

'Did he kiss you last night?' he asked

quietly.

Kerry flushed vividly. 'Certainly not!'

He smiled slightly. 'There's really no certainly not about it. You came down from the second balcony with him. He could quite easily have kissed you there.'

'Well, he didn't,' Kerry flashed back. 'He didn't dare to.'

Kelvin's smile grew at that, in spite of himself, and he shook his head.

'I think Paul Devron would be one to accept a dare rather than refuse. If he didn't kiss you, I'm inclined to think he had some other reason than being afraid to.'

Kerry scowled, thinking he was doubting her word. 'He really didn't kiss me,' she said decisively, accenting each word clearly.

Kelvin's smile grew into a laugh. 'All right, I believe you,' he assured her hastily, in mock alarm. 'I don't think any man would have the courage to kiss you—even Paul Devron.'

A reluctant smile crept over Kerry's face. 'I don't know who's the biggest fool, Kel—you or me,' she added.

He gave a mental sigh of relief. The barrier was hurdled. 'Now that the storm has died to a mere rumble in the distance, perhaps you'll tell me what all the trouble was about.' For a moment he thought he had taken the wrong opening as a mutinous look came to her face then it disappeared and she grinned. It was the old Kerry again, except for a faint restraint that wouldn't have been discernible to anyone who didn't know her so well.

'He did follow me up to the balcony, as you said. I guess he was piqued because I'd refused the prize of that stupid raffle.' The most wonderful idea came to her in a flash of inspiration. It explained everything, even to herself, and made her feel almost happy again. 'He was very nice to me, all put on, of course,' she continued, 'and I played up to him, hoping to get rid of him that way. Not that I allowed him to take any liberties.' The last was added hastily, with a quick upward glance at him. 'I thought if he had the impression that I was as moony as all the rest of them, he would lose interest and drift off. It probably worked,' she added with an assumption of carelessness that almost deceived herself. 'I don't expect we shall see him again.'

* * *

For about a week Kerry saw no more of Paul Devron. From various sources in Rylston she heard the film company was working hard and nobody had seen much of them at all in a social way. She pretended disinterest when they were mentioned, but always listened.

During that week she had managed to get herself sorted out somewhat. She could never remain a coward for long, although she might refuse to face up to the truth at once, she had at last admitted the existence of those strange feelings on the night of the ball. Still, they had passed, or nearly all of them. That was one part she was still a little reluctant to admit. Sometimes she was rather astounded to find herself wondering what it would have been like if he had kissed her on the stairs, or if she had been in the hall when the raffle was drawn.

Meantime life went on as usual. She helped Mallie around the house and also in the kitchen. In the morning there was always a lot to do and it stopped her trying to dissect her thoughts too much, but in the afternoon she often had quite a lot of spare time. That was where the danger was. She would take a book out into the wild, overgrown gardens, striving to centre her attention there and nowhere else. Sometimes she went to the large room with the wide windows and the polished floor where her mother used to dance, quietly and alone, for the sheer love of dancing. Kerry too used the room. Red hair flamed in living fire, yet the slender, girlish figure in the fluffy ballet dress had all her liquid grace. There was only one thing Kerry Derwin loved above riding—dancing. It was in her blood, dreamy and stirred by the exquisite notes of the Swan Lake ballet.

The record stopped and the enchantment was broken. Kerry came to a standstill, still on her toes. The shoes had been her mother's, but they fitted her perfectly. She had ones of her own, of course, but sometimes she liked to wear her mother's and the flimsy costumes that hung in the wardrobe. It was the one occasion she changed to feminine clothes.

She came down off her toes and walked over to the large framed and coloured picture that hung on the wall. Margaret Lambert had been a beautiful woman. She wore the very costume that her daughter, standing before her, now wore—pink shoes, white filmy ballet dress and crown of fine white feathers in her hair. The Swan Princess. To Kerry Derwin, from her earliest recollections, that picture had been one from a fairy tale. It seemed impossible that the ethereal figure could be her mother, but always she had worshipped it.

'Mother,' she whispered softly, 'I wish I'd known you.'

Then she smiled a little shamefacedly to find she had been talking to herself and crossed to the gramophone again, to turn over the record.

She was a good dancer herself, but without any finishing polish. She had herself cut short her lessons when she heard that their expense was making it hard for her father, but she still danced for the sheer love of dancing.

That was one thing she admitted she liked about Paul Devron—his dancing. Even though she might have grunted throughout the performance when she had been dragged to see his films by an eager Barbie, there had been the compensation that in some films he would dance. Even had she not been particularly interested in dancing, it would have been impossible not to appreciate and admire the sheer masculine grace of the man. They had been the only moments her eyes had been held, fascinated, on the screen. There had been one particular Argentine tango that had intrigued her from the beginning. Despite the fact that it had been almost pure sensualism and passion in dancing, she wanted to dance that tango from the first moment she saw it. Quite characteristically Kerry Derwin had not thought about what she might feel if the impossible happened and she ever did dance such a tango with Paul Devron. It was the dance itself that intrigued her, so much so that she even bought the record when the music of the soundtrack was released.

As she stood by the gramophone, Mallie came into the room. She showed no surprise at seeing Kerry in the white dress. If anything it was approval. She had been fighting a long and arduous campaign to get Kerry into skirts, so far without much success.

'Are you going into Rylston today, Miss Kerry?' she asked after a moment, her eyes still going over the whiteclad and decidedly unboyish Kerry.

'I can,' Kerry replied. It was her habit to ride into Rylston for anything they needed. 'Give me a list and I'll go as soon as I get changed.'

When Mallie had gone out again, she slipped behind the screen at the far end of the room and climbed out of the white dress and back into her riding clothes, stamped her feet down into the long boots and removed the soft white swan crown from her head. Carefully she hung the dress up in the wardrobe with the other costumes and replaced the shoes with the others in the large box in the bottom of it. Then she switched off and closed the gramophone, then went out, closing the door on the dancing white sprite who had for a time taken the place of Kerry Derwin.

Mallie handed her a short list when she reached the kitchen. 'You don't have to go straight away. They're not urgent.'

Kerry glanced at her watch and shrugged. 'I've nothing to do at the moment. I'll go and saddle Smoky.' She stuffed the list into her pocket and went out.

Joddy was weeding the garden when she passed on the way to the stable. On an impulse she stopped.

'By the way, Joddy, about the Squib. Thanks.' Her face was very solemn, but her eyes were far from that expression.

Joddy straightened up with a look of exaggerated innocence. 'The Squib, Miss Kerry? What about it?'

Kerry's mouth creased into an appreciative grin. She was not deceived.

'The three Cossacks were duly grateful.'

Joddy's blue eyes widened. 'Oh, you mean then. The Squib had wet plugs.' He blinked at her reproachfully. 'You surely don't think I did it deliberately, Miss Kerry?'

Kerry chuckled and returned his look with one of dancing glee. 'You wretch, Joddy,' she said softly. 'You know just what I mean—and thanks again.'

She didn't ride very fast away from The House. Mallie wasn't in a hurry and it was such a lovely day she took her time. It was always so easy to feel at peace out on the moors, yet today her peace didn't last for long. A few miles out from Rylston she caught sight of the film company in the distance.

For one moment she actually had an impulse to ride down there, off the trail sideways to where they were working, but she firmly restrained herself. They wouldn't want unauthorized visitors and in any case there was nobody down there she wanted to look up as a friend. The introductions that had been performed that night at the ball had been merely passing ones. Friendships wouldn't grow out of them. Of course there was nobody down there she wanted to see.

Nobody? Somewhere a demure little voice whispered in her mind and she was conscious of a startled indignation . . .

Nobody, she assured it firmly. Not even Paul Devron. Especially not Paul Devron. Then, aghast, she realized that she had been contemplating the possibility, not unpleasantly, of seeing him again.

'You're sickening for something, my girl,' she told herself grimly, and started to move away from the spot. Why on earth should she want to see Paul Devron again?

It was only when she had gone a few yards further and had not been able to resist a glance back that she suddenly realized the danger the film company was in. Even then it didn't strike her immediately. From where she was the ground dropped away sharply. For a fair distance from the foot of the hill it was comparatively flat, then it again began sloping gently. There the ground was broken and uneven. Queer little knolls thrust themselves up, tufted with long grass. At that point the narrow little track that led off the main track in the direction of the film company, split into three. None of the three were clearly defined. Valma Kent was well out on one of them.

Then she realized what was wrong.

The realization blanched her face and without hesitation she turned Smoky off the trail and down the steep side of the hill. Valma Kent was a good distance down the path. The cameras were following her at a distance, evidently getting shots of her from far off.

'The idiots!' she muttered under her breath as she rode, with an awful expectancy of seeing the fair-haired figure stumble suddenly and be sucked down in the unsuspected trap so near to her. 'Right into Gornay's Bog! Couldn't they have seen the signpost?'

As she rode, she waved to try to attract their attention. She suspected it was the most dangerous path of the three that Valma was on. Any moment she could stumble into a concealed pit.

She tried shouting, waving and shouting together and all she got in return were a few friendly waves back from those who weren't too engrossed or occupied in what was going on. Then Tom Marriott saw her coming and waved a frantic hand for her to keep back. Much as he admired the spectacle of her wild riding, it was not appreciated where it could spoil a shot.

Then at last he caught what she was saying and every drain of colour went out of his face.

'Valma's on a dangerous path!'

Lusty voices called out, irrespective of sound and cameras, Valma stopped and turned. Slowly, with infinite care, she retraced her steps. Kerry was perhaps the most tense of them all. She alone knew how very dangerous that path was. A slight deviation to either side . . . And it was not even clearly defined.

Someone else was out upon the path now, a tall man, dark in gypsyish clothes.

'It's not wide enough for two,' Kerry called after him, but Paul Devron didn't stop. The antagonism she had been fostering during the week was forgotten in the tension of the moment and she knew a sharp stab of worry.

Valma stumbled, but Paul had reached her. His hand went out and steadied her. Single file, the man close behind the white-faced actress, they regained firm ground again. It wasn't until then that everybody realized that they had been holding their breath. The sigh of relief was audible and intense.

Valma pulled herself together and smiled in answer to Tom Marriott's anxious questions.

'Yes, I'm all right. I always had a horror of quagmires, though.'

'Why didn't you tell me?' he retorted instantly. 'We could have used a double.'

'I don't believe in doubles for things I'm merely afraid of myself,' Valma answered with stubborn determination. 'If it's for something I can't do, all right, but I can walk through that bog, on the right path.'

Marriott planted his slight, wiry form in front of her and scowled. 'You'll use a double,' he growled. His tone was rough, but it wasn't irritation, although he pretended it was. There were very few who didn't have a great liking for Valma. 'That's the finish of it. You'll use a double for those shots.'

'I won't.'

It was the first time Kerry had ever seen the actress come anywhere near her own pugnaciousness, but even so she eyed them all in some amazement. Nobody seemed to be taking much notice of the fact that Valma had been so near to danger.

Smoky moved restlessly and quite suddenly felt alone and unnoticed. Everybody was watching Valma and Marriott. She was the outsider, standing on the edge of the group. She nudged Smoky and was about to turn, to leave as uninvited and unceremoniously as she had arrived, but a hand came up and stopped her. She looked down and saw that Paul Devron had come silently up behind her. Instantly she wished she had made her escape sooner.

Paul made no reference to the fact that he had arrested her movement to leave, nor did he give any sign that he had noticed her guarded stiffening.

'We all seem quite mad, don't we?' he said casually. 'Arguing about stand-ins after what nearly happened.'

Kerry felt the beginning of a smile beginning to wreck her careful expression of indifference and quickly controlled it. Was she to be so easily affected by smiling dark eyes? She had erected a barrier against the Kerry Derwin of the ball night and had vowed that it should never happen again. Was it to be torn down so quickly and easily? Was she as willing as all the others who fell victim to the smiling charm of Paul Devron?

Her lashing self-scorn erased any suspicion of a smile or even desire to smile. Make a mockery of everything she had said before—certainly not!

She affected a negligent shrug as she sat Smoky with an assumption of nonchalance she was far from feeling.

'Oh well...!' Her slightly curled lip indicated that such things were to be expected of film people.

Paul's dark eyes narrowed. So he had been right. Miss Derwin had taken herself to task for her lapse at the fancy dress ball. He should have followed up his advantage immediately by contacting her the next day, instead of giving her time to consolidate her position, but there had been too much work and he had never been one to let personal problems interfere with his work, unless it was absolutely necessary. He was rich enough not to have to worry about money if he never made another film, but Tom Marriott had a large amount sunk in the present one. He realized his responsibility as star of the film.

The smile came back to his eyes and there was lazy amusement in them as he looked up at her.

'You prickly little iceberg! Now what's wrong?'

Kerry looked away, refusing to meet his eyes. She was aware of a timbre in his voice that was almost affectionate indulgence, but she refused to let it sway her.

'Nothing that I know of,' she replied indifferently, as if it didn't matter to her one iota what he thought. 'What should be the matter?'

'That's what I'm wondering.' There was a quizzical twitch to his mouth now. You really are an amazing creature, Kerry. You've been building up a case against me during the last week, I take it. What's wrong?'

Kerry moved uneasily. His discernment both annoyed and frightened her. She didn't like to be read so easily, as if she was an open book to him.

'I don't know what you're talking about,' she replied, striving to keep the indifference intact in her voice and not sure that she was succeeding too well. Paul Devron was a man it would be hard to be indifferent to—and probably he knew it.

The last was added in an endeavour to strengthen her weakening defences with scorn directed against the besieger of them. 'Anyway,' she added, 'why should I want to build up a case against you, as you put it?'

'That's what I'd like to know.' He hid his amusement and looked at her somewhat sternly. 'Even a criminal has a chance to defend himself, Kerry.'

Kerry sought refuge in sidetracking. 'I didn't give you permission to call me Kerry,' she retorted icily.

'Then it's time you did,' he countered. 'And stop trying to look so dignified up there.' Before she could stop him, two brown hands reached up and, lifting her from the saddle with an easy strength that sent a half scared shiver through her, set her on her feet again. 'That's better. You gave me an inferiority complex perched right up there.'

A ghost of an absolutely irrepressible smile flashed across her face. 'I can't imagine you getting an inferiority complex in any circumstances,' she said, but feeling herself weaken, quickly erased the smile.

Paul sighed. 'It's on again. Young lady, if you keep this up I shall be tempted to give you reason to be really mad.'

Kerry's composure vanished in one vivid blush. Paul took one of her hands and as tugging had little, if any, effect, she had to leave it there.

'Kerry,' he said quietly, 'can't you tell me? What is it you have against me?'

Kerry swallowed hard. He was serious now and she found it difficult to stop herself weakening. Even a scornful lashing of often repeated arguments had little effect.

'Aren't you going to tell me? Is it because I'm Paul Devron?' Her glance flashed to his, startled, and he smiled and added, 'I'm not as bad as my reputation makes out, you know. Mainly it's just publicity and partly built up out of silly little incidents that meant nothing in the beginning, before rumour got at them.'

Involuntarily her smile flashed out. 'And just a few wisps of smoke that have fire as bedrock,' she said impudently.

''Fraid so,' he admitted with a rueful grimace. 'I'm only human.'

Strangely enough it was the last that broke her already damaged defences, much as she tried to repair them. The smile grew and would not be ironed out and then she was laughing. Very slowly, very carefully, the trap began to close beneath her feet.

'That's better,' he said. 'Now do you think you could bear to tell me why you don't like me?'

Kerry scuffed at a patch of grass with the toe of her polished riding boot and regarded it with concentrated attention.

'I don't really dislike you.' Her voice was very low, and she didn't look up. 'It's . . . it's just that . . . well, you're an actor and I didn't know . . .'

Her disjointed voice broke off and he took her other hand.

'I thought perhaps you were paying me back for . . . for . . . my not wanting to be kissed,' she finished in a rush.

He put a finger under her chin and tipped up her head. 'I will always be sincere with you, Kerry. Do you believe that?'

'I believe it,' she murmured, with a strange new shyness, and again her eyes fell from his, but for a different reason this time.

'As for the other matter—I always pay my debts. This one is also collecting some pretty heavy interest.'

His tone had changed. Kerry's head came up quickly and there was startled fright on her face. His expression had altered as well. The dark eyes were impudently laughing and there was a wicked tilt to the corner of his mouth. It was a Paul Devron she had seen often on the screen, when dragged there by Barbie—devil-may-care, a wealth of meaning in his too expressive black eyes. With one glance he could convey a wealth of meaning that would have been avidly sliced out by the censor if it could be put into words.

Kerry felt herself going warm all over and trembled. She knew a betraying flush had risen to her face and that he would feel her trembling through the hands he still held, but she was helpless to stop it. Even the feel of his hands on hers had changed, until she felt as if already she was held close to him, a captive to strength she had twice before had hint of. Perhaps captive also to an enchantment that was far stronger. But no, she added quickly. If that was the case, if his lips were already on hers, this breathless excitement would be heightened a thousandfold.

Then, aghast at the trend her thoughts were taking, she threw up her head defiantly.

'This is one debt you won't pay.' Her tone was as unconsciously challenging as her upflung head and had she been a little more experienced she would have realized how dangerous it was to challenge him.

His eyes danced. 'How are you going to stop me?'

His hands started a gentle but insistent tug on hers and quite inexorably she found herself drawn nearer. Panic rose in her in a racing tide. This could not be happening!

She threw a frantic glance around. Surely he wouldn't kiss her in front of everyone? Although they all seemed to have congregated in the direction of the mobile canteen, they were still in sight, despite the semi-privacy that now surrounded Paul and herself. But probably the presence of others would not worry him. He would be used to love scenes in public.

Then, just as she was becoming desperate, he released her, standing watching her with amusement.

'Don't worry. When I decide to pay that debt it won't be in front of a mob of people.' The smile grew teasing as he saw the quite patent relief that came to her face. 'And that really *was* "paying you back" for being such an icicle. So now we're quits.'

The tumult in her died down and a reluctant smile trembled on Kerry's lips. She felt she should not really smile, as that would be condoning what he had almost done, but she was powerless to stop it and he was quick to press his advantage.

'Pax?' He held out his hand, but Kerry warily kept her own at her side. 'All right.' A smile twitched at his mouth. 'I promise to behave.'

'Pax,' Kerry agreed, and her hand went out to meet his. His fingers gave it an almost impersonal pressure for one moment and then studiously released it.

'Now, to show we're friends, will you have dinner with me tomorrow night?' He saw her hesitation and added reassuringly, but with a teasing twinkle in his eyes, 'It's all quite respectable. We can have dinner at the hotel and dance there too. To make you feel quite safe I'll even invite Valma and Tom as chaperones and promise to get you home long before midnight. That do?'

Kerry smiled shyly. 'Thank you. That will do very well,' she said, rather primly, surprised and somewhat confused to find that she had her first date with Paul Devron, of all people.

'Good. I'll call for you about seven-thirty, then.' His tone became brisk. 'It seems to be eating time. Come along, you can tell us all about bogs and missing signposts now,' he added, and Kerry meekly allowed herself to be led off to the canteen.

*   *   *

Mallie had her hands in a bowl, kneading dough, with flour up to her elbows, when Kerry came into the kitchen. The girl threw herself down into a chair and stared at her polished riding boots moodily. Mallie didn't say a word; she didn't even look up. If Kerry had anything on her mind she knew well enough it would be out before long.

'Mallie,' Kerry said at last, 'what would you wear for a dinner and dance at the Galverton Hotel?'

Mallie stopped momentarily, then her hands went on kneading the soft dough as if the question was one of the sort that came from the girl every day, even though presented in a studiously careless voice. Too careless.

'Something fairly special,' she answered, obviously wondering just what Kerry was up to now.

'Oh,' Kerry answered, giving nothing away. Her brain worked at an amazing speed and came to an eminently satisfactory conclusion. 'I don't have to go, then,' she said happily. 'I haven't anything special.'

'Needn't go where, young lady?'

Kerry swung round. She found her father had unexpectedly come in from the garden and was now leaning against the doorpost. She tensed warily as he watched her with an indulgent but extremely knowing eye.

'Where have you said you'll go and now don't want to?'

She flushed under her father's too observant gaze and rose to her feet. 'Oh, nowhere in particular,' she muttered evasively and somewhat indistinctly, half knowing, though, that there was no real hope of putting him off the track.

Richard Derwin threw her a sharp glance. 'Out with it—no prevarication. What have you been up to and where don't you want to go?'

Kerry prowled the room a little uneasily. The last thing she wanted to admit was that somehow or other she had accepted a dinner engagement with Paul Devron. She scowled to herself. How on earth had she managed to get herself into such a position? It was easy enough to say no. But she had said yes. After all she had said on the subject it was humiliating to have to admit such a thing, and she felt a smouldering resentment both at her own lack of willpower and at Paul Devron for being able to persuade her.

Why hadn't she ridden straight away when the warning had been given that saved Valma Kent from the danger of the quagmire? If she had she would not now be contemplating with reluctance the thought of an evening with him.

'I said out with it,' her father's voice reminded her sternly.

Kerry moved her shoulders in a way that denoted inner rebellion. 'To dinner with Paul Devron,' she growled finally, and gave a sulky kick at the kitchen step with the toe of her boot. 'I haven't got a dress, so I can't go,' she added.

Richard Derwin straightened up off the doorpost and regarded his daughter very intently for one brief moment. He saw the mutinous twist to her lips and a mixture of other emotions that almost made him smile; almost, but not quite. He caught her by the wrist, very firmly and determinedly.

'Come along, Kerry,' he ordered. 'We're going to have a little talk.'

Kerry submitted meekly and allowed herself to be towed out of the kitchen and along the corridor that led to his study. She knew better than to resist when her father wore that expression Rick had labelled the 'lecture look'. Easy and goodnatured as he was, there were times he asserted his authority and on those occasions his recalcitrant children obeyed.

When they reached his study, he opened the door and motioned her inside. With a slightly apprehensive look she did as ordered. Here also a large framed photograph of her mother, this time smiling mischievously, hung on the wall and involuntarily Kerry smiled back, then reminded of the seriousness of the occasion, sat herself on the edge of a straight-backed chair and looked across at Richard Derwin. The man looked back, striving to keep the smile from his face. It was so unusual to see Kerry subdued and apprehensive.

'Now,' he said sternly, 'to get back to the subject of going and not going.'

Kerry swallowed hard. 'Yes?' she

questioned meekly.

'To begin with, there was no compulsion whatever on you to accept this invitation, I take it?' he asked.

She struggled with a cowardly and very dishonest impulse to say yes, there was and she had been shamefully coerced, but in the end her natural pride and self-respect won.

'No. I said yes quite freely,' she added.

He watched her unrelentingly. 'And now you don't want to go?'

Kerry shifted about in the chair and a trifle sulkily looked down at her hands. 'I don't know,' she muttered.

'That's no reason.' He sat down at his desk and turned so that he could still look at her fully. 'Don't you like Paul Devron?'

This was getting on dangerous ground. Kerry wished she could avoid answering that one, but knowing her father she realized there was not a hope. He would have an answer and a truthful one at that.

'No . . .' she said, and wouldn't look at him. 'Yes . . . I mean, I don't know,' she amended confusedly. 'I like him when I'm with him, but afterwards I sort of change round.' The admission was made with the utmost reluctance, the first part at least.

For a moment Richard Derwin was

silent. He rose to his feet and went to the window to look out. Kerry also remained quiet and wished she could guess what he was thinking. Then he turned and walked over until he stood over her.

'What I think is the matter with you, young lady,' he said with quiet scorn she didn't know was assumed, 'is just sheer cowardice. You're afraid of receiving a few teasing remarks on having your first date after all your remarks on the subject. Is that it?'

Kerry's eyes flashed. 'No!' she denied hotly, and flushed a fiery red. 'It's not that at all. Anyway,' she added, 'you seem strangely determined to have me go out with a man you've never met and with a reputation like Paul Devron has.'

Richard Derwin's own eyes flashed. 'You're still not too old to get a spanking, young Kerry. As for Paul Devron, although I've never met him, I have spoken quite lengthily to Colonel Treveryl on the subject and I'm prepared to trust his judgment. He likes and trusts Paul Devron. Did you think I would encourage you to go out with anybody I knew nothing about—especially after what happened at the ball,' he ended.

Kerry flushed again. 'Nothing happened at the ball.'

He slanted her a sideways look. 'And you can thank Paul Devron for that,' he retorted. 'That raffle was all in the spirit of fun and it would have served you right if he'd kissed you in front of everybody when he returned. The papers made quite a joke out of it at his expense.'

Kerry looked up, startled. 'Did they?'

'Of course they did. If you troubled to read the papers you would realize that, when they arrive, of course,' he added, remembering the somewhat spasmodic arrival of newspapers at The House and the fact that he had heard most of it from Colonel Treveryl.

'What did they say?' Kerry asked in a very small voice.

'Oh, the usual things.' He made a vague gesture. ' "Hollywood's top lover flattened by Devon Moors girl"—"Paul Devron gets a no".' He shrugged. 'Oh, they had great fun out of the situation and he was game enough to take it. Now it's your turn. Maybe you'll be teased, but how do you imagine he felt when that film company doubtless started on him?'

Kerry contemplated the matter. It hadn't

occurred to her before that Paul had probably had to put up with a lot more than she would if she went on with this dinner engagement. If? There seemed to be no doubt about it. Honour bound her to go. Not only honour. Surely there was some pleasure in it. She refused to go any further from there though.

'I'm sorry,' she said with an apologetic glance up at her father. 'I . . . I suppose it's just because I'm shy of . . . well, he's a complete stranger.'

Derwin laughed and put an arm affectionately around her shoulders. 'Of course. Every girl dies, or so I'm told. You're growing up now. It's quite natural that you'll find yourself changing, in spite of your scornful views on the subject of romance.'

Kerry's head went up and the familiar pugnacious look came to her chin. 'I'm not changing,' she flashed. 'I still think the same.'

Her father's eyes twinkled. 'Of course,' he agreed hastily. 'However, that shouldn't stop you going out and enjoying yourself. You like dancing, don't you, and from what I hear Paul Devron is an excellent dancer.'

Kerry hesitated. She felt like a pendulum. There was still the old reluctance in the background that didn't want to lower the flag of scorn and at the same time a strange fear of the dark magnetism of him. On the other end of the swing of the pendulum was her love of dancing and the infectious amusement that could be in his eyes, when they didn't have impudent devilry that could set her nerves thrilling, even against the banner of her scorn.

It would have been hard to make a decision, but for the other matter.

'I still don't have a dress,' she pointed out, and wondered if what she felt was relief or really disappointment.

'Oh!' An expression of blank dismay crossed his face. Male-like he hadn't thought of that. 'Nothing at all that would do for the occasion?' he inquired hopefully.

Kerry shook her head instantly. That question needed very little time to settle. She had exactly two dresses. One was too small and even so it was only a cotton washing frock that had once been blue and had now faded to a peculiar white-grey. The other was a particularly livid shade of purple that had been chosen for her by her aunt, now deceased, with no eye for colour. That was silk, but . . . Kerry shuddered as she thought of it.

'Neither of them would do,' she said. 'Neither of them fits me,' she added as an afterthought.

Richard Derwin rumpled up his hair rather bewilderedly. 'We'll just have to get you one then.'

Kerry shook her head. 'No,' she said sternly. 'We can't afford it.' They had always been truthful about money matters in the Derwin household. It helped to know the exact state of the exchequer so that no unnecessary little luxuries or extravagances were indulged in.

''Fraid you're right there.' He scratched his chin reflectingly. 'Those darn shares just recently took another turn for the worse too, so we'll have to economize even more in the future.'

Kerry gave him a dismayed look and thought of one or two little things that now seemed unnecessary luxuries.

'Why didn't you tell me? I said a long while ago I should get a proper job. I definitely shall get some kind of a job,' she announced firmly, without any idea at all of what sort. 'Mallie needs no help in running this place.'

'We'll probably have to think about it,' he admitted reluctantly. 'But anyway, not right at this moment. The present problem seems to be to find you something to wear.' He broke off and began to pace the floor thoughtfully. Suddenly he stopped and flashed round with a boyish exclamation of triumph that quite startled her. 'Got it! One of your mother's ballet dresses.' As she blinked in surprise, he caught hold of her hand and pulled her up. 'Come on. We'll go and investigate.'

Enthusiastically interested in his own idea, he towed her up the stairs after him and threw open the door into the dance room. Marching across the smooth floor, he then surveyed the rows of costumes with a speculative eye.

Kerry, becoming interested herself, pulled out a costume that was a favourite of hers. It had the usual, graceful floating skirt and a bodice of white satin trimmed with tiny white feathers. The narrow little shoulder straps were also made of joined white feathers.

'Go and put it on,' her father instructed, excited as a boy over his brainwave, and while she disappeared behind the screen, he rummaged around among the shoes and found a pair of silver ones, made to imitate ballet shoes but with the soles of ordinary shoes. 'Even solved the shoe question,' he called out. 'Your mother had a pair made that looked like ballet shoes, but which were more comfortable to wear for parties after shows.'

Kerry came from behind the screen and he studied her for a moment in approving silence.

He swallowed hard and shook his head. 'Yes, you're growing up, Kerry.' There was sadness in his voice for the loss of his madcap daughter, but pride in the new Kerry that was slowly replacing her.

Kerry looked a bit surprised at his expression, but decided not to comment on it.

'Will it do?' she asked anxiously.

'It'll do very well,' he assured her, and felt it to be a vast understatement.

She peered down and tugged somewhat ineffectually at the top of the dress. 'It's rather bare.'

'Don't be silly,' he retorted. 'It's far more decent than the majority of evening dresses. Anyway, you've worn it before when you've been dancing up here.'

'That's different,' she objected with what her father thought typical feminine logic. 'I didn't have to go out in it.'

'You're not used to evening dresses, that's all, or wearing any type of dresses, come to that.' He paused and then added thoughtfully, 'There's a little lace jacket you can wear. It's downstairs. I'll get it for you later. You'll need something over your shoulders anyway when you go out, even though it looks like being warm tomorrow as well as today. We shall probably have a good summer this year.'

Kerry didn't even blink at his surprising change of subject. She was quite used to him suddenly going off on to another track.

'And now, having settled your problems for you,' he continued, 'I take it I may return to my writing. I have my heroine in a very awkward situation and she'll take a lot more extricating than you did!'

Kerry grinned as she watched him go out. Already he had an absent look on his face. She knew that she was probably half forgotten by now. It always happened that way. Quite suddenly he would descend to or depart from reality and that was that until the spasm had passed.

She went behind the screen and changed

back to her usual clothes. Her mind started to drift back to one of the things her father had said.

Was she a coward? Was her reluctance to keep her appointment for tomorrow connected with a desire to avoid the teasing she knew she would have to face? Quite certainly she knew there would be teasing. It was inevitable. After her oft-repeated remarks about love, love scenes and Paul Devron in particular, both her friends and those who only professed friendship, to which latter category she was beginning to believe Merle Connors belonged, would be ready with not only teasing but also malicious remarks.

There was one thing, however, that Kerry Derwin was not, and that was a coward. Let them talk, she decided, with a pugnacious set to her chin. She liked dancing and Paul Devron was an excellent dancer. She could no longer accuse him of conceit and he could be an amusing and entertaining companion, even though, she reminded herself, it was sometimes spiced with the scent of danger.

CHAPTER FOUR

'MISS KERRY!' Mallie rapped on Kerry's door. 'He's here!'

Kerry opened the door, wrapped in her blue dressing gown, and was treated to the spectacle of a flushed and excited Mallie.

'Who's here?' she asked impishly.

Mallie blushed like a schoolgirl. 'Paul Devron.'

The wicked grin that Mallie knew so well turned Kerry's lips. 'Why, Mallie,' she crowed delightedly, 'I believe you've fallen for him!'

Mallie bridled. 'Certainly not!' she denied. 'At my age!' She came in and shut the door after her. 'You'd better let me help you dress.'

Kerry threw off the dressing gown and appeared clad in a neat tailored and strapless slip that had been unearthed from among her mother's former belongings. They were both of almost the same size and only a few minor alterations had made it fit her perfectly.

She sat down on a chair and began to pull on fine tights in a way that made Mallie shudder.

'Careful, child,' she objected quickly. 'You'll ladder them.'

Kerry's ruthless, tugging fingers ceased and she looked up with a rueful grimace. 'They're such darn fragile things. Father presented me with these this morning.'

The next step was to lace up the shoes, an easy enough procedure that presented no unaccustomed difficulties whatever, and then Mallie was lifting the white dress. It slid over her head, billowing out from her waist in soft, misty waves as Mallie patted it into place and clipped up the back opening.

Again Kerry peered down. 'It's a bit low,' she protested for the second time, her head bent and hands tugging at the dress. She hated to admit it, but she was more than a little shy of appearing before Paul dressed as she was. Before she had always had the refuge of her boyishness to protect her, first the Cossack costume and then her trim riding clothes. Now she most definitely looked a girl and the dress showed far more of her than she was used to showing in public.

'Don't be silly,' said Mallie. 'You wear swimming suits.'

Kerry scowled. 'That's different.' She

snatched up the little lace jacket and put it on. The scowl died. She felt more dressed. 'That's better.'

It took away the bare look to her satisfaction but, Mallie noted with approval, it didn't make her look any less feminine and lovely.

Kerry ran a careless comb through her hair and was again stopped by Mallie.

'Do it properly,' she was instructed.

Kerry looked blank. 'How? I always comb it properly.'

Mallie took the comb and brush away from her. She brushed and combed and pulled and pinned until Kerry began to get impatient.

'That will be good enough,' she protested at one stage, and was firmly silenced by Mallie.

'It isn't good enough!' Mallie had been the nearest to a mother Kerry had ever known and on occasion she transferred from being the housekeeper to treating Kerry almost as her own daughter. 'Most girls would look forward to going out with a man as attractive as Paul Devron and would try to make themselves look as nice as possible. I know you like to consider yourself different from most girls . . .' here

Kerry opened her mouth to protest, but Mallie went on quite unheedingly, 'but you've accepted his invitation and you might at least take the trouble to take some trouble over it,' she said, managing to get rather mixed towards the end.

Kerry didn't seem to notice the mix-up. It was the sort of thing she would probably have said herself.

She looked a little apologetic. 'I'm sorry, Mallie. I sound awfully conceited.' She broke off and looked down at her hands shyly. 'I really am looking forward to it, though. It's . . . it's just that . . . well, that I'm not used to it.'

Mallie beamed at her, quite mollified. 'Of course you're not, but you will be. You like him, don't you?'

Kerry nodded. 'Oh yes.' She spoke quite involuntarily and then with surprise realized the truth of the words. She really did like him. It wasn't only the dancing. She was looking forward to seeing Paul again.

Mallie finished with combs and pins and straightened up. 'Now you stay right there,' she ordered. 'I haven't finished yet and I don't want you to get a look at yourself until I have.'

She crossed to the door and went out. Kerry watched her with frowning eyes, glad of a few minutes to herself, especially in view of the astounding truth of her reply to Mallie's question.

It was most confusing to find how her liking for Paul Devron had grown quietly by itself, when she had been telling herself all along that she didn't like him and was really not at all interested in him. It was all most confusing.

Somewhat intrigued, she began to investigate that liking. It had begun with antagonism on the balcony on the night of the fancy dress ball, but had changed halfway through to a partly wary sparring and then to the complete enchantment that she had once denied existed. Of course, even now, she still denied it, but it had been pleasant sparring with him.

And the second instance, on the moors, when she had ridden to warn Valma Kent of danger. That too had started in the same way—antagonism and then liking.

Once away from him she had again almost overcome the liking, although why for the life of her she should want to she couldn't understand now. She had never tried to kill her liking for Kelvin Treveryl.

But that was different. Just what the difference was, though, she didn't know.

Perhaps she feared Paul Devron. Then again—why? He'd never given her cause to fear him, but it might be that instinctively she sensed the hunter behind the impudent challenge his dark eyes so often held, a challenge that was never there with Kelvin Treveryl.

This time, though, she had not succeeded in killing her liking, even though that instinctive, hidden fear might still be there.

Mallie came back to find her still sitting in the chair with every sign of not having moved and she nodded approvingly.

'You haven't looked?' Kerry dutifully assured her she hadn't moved and Mallie laid a small leather case on the table. 'Good. I haven't finished with you yet.'

She peered curiously at the box Mallie was opening. 'What is it?'

'A make-up kit. Your father went into Rylston for it this morning.'

Kerry frowned. 'Oh, he shouldn't have,' she said in quick dismay. 'He knows we can't really afford things like that.'

'Be still, child,' Mallie said firmly. 'And don't say anything like that to him, to take his pleasure out of it.'

'I promise,' she said meekly. 'I really do like it, but I've never worn make-up. Do I really have to use it?'

'With that dress you do,' Mallie assured her. She raked in the case, pulling the contents out interestedly. 'I wonder if he managed to get the right shade. He probably got one of the girls in the store to help him. You're well known in Rylston.'

Kerry grinned. Sometimes the opinion was that she was too well known in Rylston.

Mallie finished her inspection of the box's contents and nodded in satisfaction. 'It's the right colour.' She frowned slightly as she looked at Kerry. 'I suppose I shall have to let you see something of yourself to put this on.'

Kerry smiled beguilingly, entering into the fun of the thing. 'I won't look properly,' she promised, but nevertheless the moment she caught sight of her head and shoulders in the mirror and what Mallie had done to her hair, she let out a startled exclamation.

'Mallie! It won't stay like that.'

'It will,' Mallie said firmly. 'Leave it alone and don't go pulling out the pins.'

She was instructed to remove the lace jacket and under Mallie's surprisingly expert guidance was shown how to apply a light dusting of powder and a thin film of lipstick.

'No more,' Mallie adjured her. 'You only want a faint suspicion of it.'

Kerry gave her a look compounded of surprised admiration and curiosity. 'You sound like an authority on the subject,' she commented.

'I was young myself once,' Mallie replied dryly. 'Shut your eyes and stand up.'

Kerry did as instructed and felt herself led over in the direction of the full-length mirror.

'Now open your eyes.'

She did so—and gasped. A stranger stared back at her, a stranger that was life and the impetuous flame of youth. Softly, golden tanned shoulders rose out of the white bodice of the dress that hugged the young tender curves of her breasts. The tiny, soft white feathers clung to her smooth, clear skin with an affectionate intimacy and there was another narrow band of them around one of the slender, graceful arms. From the slim waist, the drifting white skirt billowed out, allowing a glimpse of neat ankles and small, silver-shod feet. But the face of the stranger was equally startling, framed by flaming hair that was drawn back from either side of her face. Her mouth, faintly outlined by the lipstick, was young and innocently enticing.

The startled green eyes turned to Mallie. 'Is that me?' a small voice asked.

'It is,' Mallie assured her. 'Now go and enjoy yourself—and don't be afraid of him.'

Kerry, about to move off, stopped dead on the spot. 'I'm not afraid of him!' she flashed indignantly, then stopped and considered the statement. 'Anyway, even if I had been, which I'm not, why did you tell me not to?'

Mallie in turn considered the rather involved question. 'Because, deep down, he could never do anything to make a girl afraid of him,' she said finally.

'How do you know?' Kerry's eyes were curious.

'A woman is supposed to know those things by instinct, but anyway you can see it in him, even speaking to him for just a moment. Even on the screen, all those actors and actresses manage to put across something of their real personality. That's why there are those you can never like, however good an actor they appear and whatever parts they play.'

'Oh!' Her voice was very thoughtful.

'And another thing,' Mallie added, 'a good-looking girl can always twist a man around her little finger if she knows how to go about it.'

An impish smile flitted across Kerry's face for one moment. 'Are you suggesting that I try it on Paul Devron?' She had an idea that she would get more than she bargained for if she did.

'You'd come to no harm, but you'd probably get more than you bargained for,' Mallie replied. 'Now you'd better go down. It's nearly eight, Miss Kerry,' she went on, with a return to her housekeeper manner.

Kerry picked up the little lace jacket and drew it on, fighting a new shyness that threatened to descend on her.

'Thank you for helping me, Mallie,' she almost whispered as she swallowed a gigantic lump in her throat.

She opened the door and walked slowly to the top of the stairs, with the housekeeper behind her. As she took the first step downwards the door into her father's study opened and he and Paul Devron came out together. Both were smiling and seemed to have become exceedingly friendly in the short time they had been together. Then some slight sound made both of them look towards the stairs. Kerry was too far away to see the sudden, swift fire that leapt into Paul's eyes and then came quickly under control.

As she descended the stairs, in spite of the ridiculous shyness, she found her eyes drawn to him, savouring with a strange new appreciation how attractive he was. He was wearing a dinner jacket that showed his slim yet powerful body to advantage and the dark hair shone like polished jet. One hand was raised, resting on the post at the bottom of the stairway as he watched her coming down towards him. His lips were smiling and his eyes had such an intent regard that she felt a warm flush run up into her face.

'I'm sorry to have kept you waiting,' she murmured, hearing her voice descend to a confused whisper.

The smiling appreciation in his eyes deepened as they went over her and came back to her face. 'The result was worth waiting for.'

Kerry felt the warmth in her cheeks increasing. Desperately she dug her toes into her silver slippers in the hope that might counteract the blush, as someone had once told her it would, but it was a vain hope. It would be hard to find something to counteract eyes that said so many things and hinted at others. She felt a shivery excitement inside her and was glad of the little lace jacket that covered the, to her, too revealing dress.

Paul took her hand and placed it on his arm and a little tingle went through her at his touch. 'I promise to have her back before twelve,' he said to Richard Derwin. His glance went to Kerry with a hint of teasing. 'Or she may change into a swan princess before my very eyes!'

Richard Derwin laughed. 'You'd better clip her wings. She has no bow and arrows tonight, or Cossack accoutrements hidden away, though, so I think she's quite safe.' He watched them through the doorway, then firmly closed the door and kept Mallie, who showed signs of wishing to peep through the curtains, fully occupied.

Paul opened the door of the black car and helped Kerry in. He then went quickly around to the other side and slid in beside her. The door closed, shutting them into the peculiar intimacy of the small confines of a saloon car, and Kerry was overwhelmingly conscious of his proximity, more so as he leaned slightly towards her.

'I wonder if he was right?' he mused.

'Who?'

'Your father.' A finger under her chin tipped her head up, so that she had to look at him. 'He said you're quite safe tonight, but I'm not so sure. I would say you're far more dangerous.'

Kerry swallowed hard and gave him a wary look. She didn't quite understand what he meant, but she sensed they were approaching dangerous ground and took refuge in bewilderment.

'What do you mean?' she asked, and looked quite unconvincingly innocent. 'I don't understand.'

'Don't you?' He sounded amused. 'It doesn't matter. You will one day.' He reached behind him and handed her a cellophane box. Kerry flashed a quick, startled look and then opened it and took out two pale orchids. Very carefully she turned them in awed fingers. It was the first time anyone had ever given her flowers.

'Are they orchids?' she asked wonderingly.

Paul threw her an amused glance as he started the car. 'They are. Do you like them?'

'They're lovely.' She touched the stiff, exotic petals gently. A swift, shy glance met his briefly and then dropped again. 'Thank you, Paul.'

He was silent for a moment, negotiating a difficult part of the road that was a road by name only, but she could see that he was smiling.

'You're unusually amenable tonight, my child. I expected you to be bristling with thistles as usual.'

Kerry sat upright. She had all the very young's resentment of being called a child. 'I'm not a child,' she informed him stiffly. 'I'm eighteen.'

'So very old!' His voice had a teasing inflection. 'Am I to infer from that remark that you don't wish to be treated as a child?' He glanced at her sideways and what little light there was showed his eyes to be dancing. It was the same look she had met when she had run from him to the balcony on the night of the ball. It was the impudent, devil-may-care look of the moors encounter, the wicked lilt was back to his voice. 'On second thoughts, though,' he continued, 'I'm inclined to think the "child" part was merely a slip of the tongue. There's nothing of the child about you tonight. In fact very much the opposite.'

Kerry swallowed hard and threw him another wary look. She contemplated sliding further along the seat, away from him, but didn't attempt it, fearing it might bring retaliation on her unsophisticated but quite understanding head.

'Well,' he said, 'I'm still waiting for an answer to my question.'

'What question?' she countered suspiciously.

'Was that an invitation not to treat you as a child?' The teasing amusement was still in his voice.

Kerry, realizing she was skating on very thin ice, didn't quite know how to answer him. She was beginning to realize that to dare or challenge him was a dangerous thing.

'I meant that I didn't want to be treated as a child,' she began, trying to choose her words very carefully, so that a double meaning couldn't be read into them, 'but I didn't want to . . . to . . .' It was no use. She broke off, unable to continue, and a warm and very betraying flush stained her cheeks.

Paul laughed. 'I know exactly what you mean. What a frightened little innocent you are, Kerry darling!'

Kerry felt something like an electric shock go through her at the unexpected endearment, then she reminded herself quickly that he probably said it so often, on and off the screen, it was quite casual and unconscious, in fact quite meaningless too.

Before she had quite recovered from the shock of that, Paul reached out and, with a cool audacity that gave no warning of his intention, took possession of one of the hands lying lightly clasped in her lap and drew it up to rest beneath his on the steering wheel.

Kerry gave a gasp and made an ineffectual attempt to tug it free. 'Let go of me!' she said indignantly.

'No,' he retorted with unambiguous simplicity, but the impudent amusement was still in his voice.

Kerry tugged at her hand again. It was altogether too disturbing to leave it where it was. The fingers under his were tingling in a most peculiar way. She tugged again, but his grip only tightened.

'Don't be such a thistle,' he said. 'Or I'll give you something to be really cross about.'

Very quickly she became still. There had been a warning in his voice and she was under no misapprehension what he meant. Much as she longed to continue the fight, she had to leave her hand there, unresisting, and the sensations it aroused in her were altogether too disquieting for her peace of mind. The tingle was definitely growing worse. It was spreading through her whole body. The road was so bad it necessitated a really firm hold upon the wheel and that meant her hand as well. The pressure of his fingers wasn't at all light or impersonal and now and again she was thrown against him as the car jolted on the uneven surface of the road.

'You promised to behave,' a very small voice reminded him.

'That was on another occasion,' he retorted. 'And anyway, I consider that I'm behaving with remarkable restraint, especially in view of some of the things I would like to do.'

Very wisely Kerry kept silent. He was

too experienced, too much a man of the world, for her to have a hope of winning. He would have an answer to everything she said. Yet, strangely, she couldn't bring back her initial dislike of him. Something kept it at bay.

Surreptitiously she glanced sideways at him. In the darkness his profile was distinctly aquiline and even a little ruthless. It was the face of a man used to getting his own way, used to giving orders and having them obeyed. If he really set his mind to anything he would be quite ruthless in obtaining it. With a little shiver of fear she wondered what he wanted of her—and with a flash of insight wondered also whether she would be strong enough to withstand him.

He kept her hand prisoner until they reached the main road and then in a surprisingly short time they were drawing up outside the brightly lit hotel. With Paul's hand beneath her elbow they entered the foyer, and Kerry was strangely disappointed to discover that Valma Kent and Tom Marriott were to be present after all. Somehow she found herself carried off by the actress into the ladies' powder room. She carefully combed up a few stray ends of hair, aware all the time of Valma's eyes on her. When she finally turned round, Valma smiled.

'You look very nice tonight, Kerry.'

Kerry dropped her eyes shyly. 'Thank you.' She heard Valma laugh and looked up again.

'You know, I think you rather surprised Paul,' the actress commented. 'He expected you to find some excuse not to come.'

Her quick, gamin grin flashed out irresistibly. 'I nearly didn't,' she admitted.

Valma eyed her with frank curiosity. 'Why? Don't you like him?'

Kerry moved a trifle uneasily. She could no longer say quite truthfully that she disliked him, but on the other hand she couldn't bring herself to admit aloud that she did like him. In the end she fell back on her old standby.

'Well, he plays such silly parts,' she said childishly. 'All that lovemaking.' Nevertheless her upward glance was a little defiant.

'Are they really such silly parts?' Valma questioned after a pause, very quietly and seriously. 'Paul does have a gift, you know, and he's quite unconceited about it, although he knows that he possesses it. It would be impossible for him not to. You think that love is a lot of nonsense, and you're quite entitled to your opinion,' she added hastily, expecting interjections from Kerry, 'but the majority of women don't. There are many of them unloved in the world, many who have made unhappy marriages, who have given their love where it's not wanted, or are too plain to ever hope that they will be loved. Do you think it's silly if Paul's gift can bring happiness to them for a little while? It's doing no harm, and everyone likes to live in a dream world for a little while. Even apart from those unhappy ones, there are the young ones, in love, who can appreciate his acting; it makes them think of their boy-friend. And there are those who go just for the entertainment or pleasure a film gives them. After all, it's a woman's right to be loved—even if it's only in a dream world and for a little while.'

Kerry stared at her wonderingly. She had never thought of it like that before. She would probably not be quite so intolerant of Barbie's sighs next time.

'So you see, it isn't as silly as it seems to you,' Valma finished with a smile that took all offence out of her following remark. 'Not all women are cold little fishes like you.'

Kerry didn't speak, although she was beginning to be a little uncertain whether Valma's last remark was strictly true. If she still was a 'cold little fish', what right had her fingers to tingle as they had done at Paul's touch?

To take her mind off it, she picked up the spray of orchids and was about to indicate that she was ready to join the others when Valma nodded towards the exotic flowers.

'Take off your jacket and pin them to your dress,' she suggested. 'You can leave the jacket here.'

Kerry flushed and hastily pinned the flowers on to the lace jacket. 'No, I think I'll keep it on.'

Valma guessed instantly what the flush meant. 'There's no need to be frightened or shy of Paul.' She smiled mischievously. 'Forget he's Paul Devron. He's only a man, and a pretty girl can make a man do just what she wants if she knows how to go about it.'

A smile twitched at Kerry's lips. 'Even Paul Devron?'

She went thoughtfully silent for a moment. Two people had said that to her—first Mallie, now Valma. But would she dare, especially in view of what the consequences might be? Paul was rather dangerous fire to play with. Nevertheless a mischievous impishness began to well up in her.

'But I wouldn't know . . .' she began.

Valma's eyes twinkled. 'Don't you believe it. A girl knows those things instinctively. And now shall we join our escorts who, although they like to think they're rather important, are after all mere men,' she finished with a note of conspiratorial laughter in her voice.

Kerry's eyes danced in sympathy and together they went out. Male and female heads alike turned to watch them as they passed. The tall sophisticated, self-assured woman with her exquisite fair beauty they recognized instantly. Most Rylstonites present had difficulty in placing the slender flame of a girl at her side, and they gasped when they did.

Valma was wearing a black gown that was the masterpiece of some artist and the drifting mistiness of Kerry's ballerina dress was a perfect foil for it. One was a cool goddess of beauty, the other from some ancient fairytale, and neither detracted from but rather enhanced the other.

Marriott and Paul rose to their feet as they approached, both of them appreciating the picture the woman and the young girl made.

A waiter led them to a reserved table in the best position in the room and then another was waiting to take their order. When it came to her turn to order, Kerry stared at the menu blankly, then inspiration came. She did what she had seen on the screen, so many times—handed the menu to Paul.

'Will you order for me, please?'

Without a sign of surprise he did so, then turned back to her when the waiter had gone.

'How do you know you'll like what I order?'

Kerry read the double meaning in his words and an impish sparkle came to her eyes.

'I'm sure I should like whatever you ordered,' she answered with an unbelievably innocent expression.

He shot her a quizzical glance. 'Everything?'

Her eyes danced as the innocent look disappeared and puckish laughter took its place. 'Well—within reason.' Then she caught Valma's eye and both of them burst out laughing.

The two men looked at them warily. 'What have you two been hatching?' Marriott asked.

Valma turned her large blue eyes on him. 'Nothing,' she said, looking innocent and making a better job of it than Kerry had. She then looked at Kerry and spoilt the effect when both of them laughed.

'I have an idea she's been instructing young Kerry in a few women's wiles,' Paul commented with mock grimness. 'Heaven help us now with the pair of them!'

'Serves you right,' Valma said complacently. 'It's our only defence.' She glanced at Kerry. 'Don't forget what I told you.'

Paul intercepted a sparkling glance between the two and eyed the actress suspiciously. 'Just what have you two been talking about?'

Kerry felt the bubbling excitement going to her head. Mallie and Valma had been right. For the first time she sensed a feeling of power and imagined herself in complete command of the situation.

She reached out and patted his hand lightly, consolingly. 'About you, of course, but don't worry,' she said with a daring she wouldn't previously have thought herself capable of.

'You, young lady, are asking for trouble,' Paul told her with a warning glint in his eyes. He rose to his feet suddenly and pulled her up with him. 'Come and dance. That will take some of the fight out of you.'

He was right. As soon as they were on the floor, separated from the other two, with his arms around her, Kerry felt her new courage and audacity oozing away. It went steadily and quite inexorably. She felt very small and very much alone with him, despite the crowded floor. He was holding her closely, more so than the dance really permitted, and his dark cheek was against her hair.

'Not so full of retorts now, are you?' he jeered, as she tried to draw away from him. 'Look up at me, you little coward.'

Kerry steadfastly kept her head bent. She knew she was definitely not in control of the situation now. Very much to the contrary. As when dancing with him before, she was conscious of his tall, slim body against hers and the hand on her back was moving slightly with a caressing movement. His head was bent now and his cheek was resting against hers, even though she tried to turn her head away. Once she knew his lips lightly touched the fiery hair where it sprang away from the smooth skin. It was only the ghost of a caress, but she felt it with every nerve in her body.

'How . . . how dare you!' she stammered breathlessly.

'Dare I what?' he questioned.

'Kiss me!'

'I didn't.'

'You did,' she retorted indignantly. 'I felt it.'

'That wasn't a kiss.' His tone was still jeering. 'You'll feel it a lot more when I really do kiss you.'

Kerry was about to reply hotly that he had better not try at any time, but wisely refrained. He would be quite capable of either kissing her in front of everyone, or manoeuvring her out into the gardens and proving whether or not he dared to.

After that they danced in silence. He still held her closely and his cheek still rested against hers. Rebellious, but utterly helpless, she submitted.

When at last the dance ended he led her off the floor. Bending his head, he whispered: 'Still want to cross swords with me?'

Kerry, to her astonishment, discovered she did.

As soon as they sat down again, she noticed Tom Marriott watching her speculatively. She didn't think anything of it at first, but as the evening proceeded it was impossible to ignore it any longer, and at last she flashed him an inquiring glance.

'Miss Derwin, have you ever thought of doing any acting?'

His words took her quite unawares. She shook her head dumbly, wondering what was on his mind.

Paul glanced at her quizzically. 'He's about to offer you a part in our present film.'

Kerry blinked dazedly and looked from one to the other of them uncomprehendingly.

'I don't understand. Why me?'

'I'll be quite frank, Miss Derwin,' Marriott began. 'To begin with, we had Rita Lane, but we had to suspend her because she became too temperamental. The next we heard she had found a legal flaw in her contract and managed to get out of it. By that time we'd already started filming. She knew it would cost us time and consequently money to replace her and I think she hoped to come back more or less on her own terms. We've gone almost as far as we can and up to now we hadn't found anyone suitable. The part has to be filled very soon.'

'But why me?' Kerry repeated. It just wouldn't sink in, and what part had managed to penetrate seemed unbelievable. 'I can't act.'

'How do you know?' he retorted. 'I have a hunch that you'll be able to play the part. Not only that, I saw you ride the day of the fancy dress dance. I want a girl who can ride like that for the part. Rita could dance, but we would have had to teach her to ride.'

'How do you know I can dance? You can't tell from just watching me dance on this crowded floor.' Something was making her find difficulties. The thought of acting in a film with Paul Devron was disturbing.

'Paul has danced with you. He can tell whether you'll make a dancer.'

'I've had some dancing lessons,' she admitted at last, shyly. 'This is one of my mother's ballet dresses I'm wearing now.'

He went on quickly, 'Then what have you got to be afraid of? You'll agree to take the part?'

Kerry made a bewildered gesture. She couldn't understand why she should be offered such a chance.

'I thought it was terribly hard to get a part in a film, but you're actually trying to persuade me to take it,' she said with a helpless gesture.

'Tom is playing a hunch,' Valma put in. She leaned forward and touched the younger girl's hand encouragingly. 'Chance it, Kerry. We'll have to test you first, of course, but we need somebody for the part of Metani and Tom's hunches usually come out right.'

'Metani?' Kerry questioned.

'Metani, the witch girl,' Paul answered with a smile. 'It's a period film, set a couple of hundred years ago. Metani lives on the moors and claims that she can remember hundreds of years ago when she rode by the side of Queen Boadicea, in another part of Britain, and fought against the Roman soldiers.'

Kerry's eyes lit up. The slight element of fantasy in it appealed to her. She completely forgot, for the moment, that being a Paul Devron film it would probably be heavily laced with love scenes, some of which would involve her. Rita Lane was not a small part actress.

Kerry was wavering, and then another aspect of it appeared to her. The Derwin household was short of funds and she would be paid for the role, probably well paid. She had wanted to take a job of some kind and this had come straight from heaven. Even if she didn't want to accept, which was not strictly true, out of consideration for her family she shouldn't refuse.

What mainly held her back was the fear that she couldn't do it. Actors and actresses had seemed a remote race, seen and heard only per the medium of the cinema and even when met in person, beings apart. It would be more than strange to find herself becoming one of them. It would be like entering a new world, but she knew quite suddenly that she would accept.

'All right,' she said. 'If you're prepared to take the chance, I am too.'

'Good girl,' Paul said briefly. He filled her glass from a bottle that had appeared on the table while they were dancing. 'This calls for a celebration.'

Kerry regarded the sparkling liquid suspiciously. 'What is it?'

'Champagne,' Valma replied. 'What do we drink to?'

Paul lifted his glass. 'To Metani,' he said, and smiled at Kerry.

She watched them drink theirs but was rather wary of her own. Finally, under their amused eyes, she picked it up and sipped slowly. With a grimace of distaste she put the glass down.

'I don't like it.'

Tom Marriott laughed. 'Everybody likes champagne.'

Kerry lifted the glass again and took another sip. Mallie had accused her of wanting to be different from everybody else and the accusation had made her feel vaguely ashamed, as if she was being conceited. If everybody else liked champagne, she would have a try at liking it.

It was no use, though. 'I still don't like it,' she announced. Her eyes regarded Tom Marriott sternly. 'Do you really like it?'

He gave her a conspiratorial wink. 'Well, to be quite truthful, I don't,' he admitted ruefully.

'Well...' Kerry put her glass down

with a decided air, as if that clinched the matter. 'Please, I would rather have lemonade,' she requested, not caring whether she sounded gauche and schoolgirlish.

'Drink it up,' Valma said persuasively. 'Just this once. It won't hurt you. Drink to the success of the film.'

With an expression of great distaste she managed to drink a few more mouthfuls, and set the glass down again, still half full.

'Now, will you come and dance with me?' Tom Marriott asked. 'That's if Paul doesn't decide to challenge me to mortal combat.'

Paul looked up with a lazy smile. 'Not if you don't try to monopolize her.'

Kerry, dancing with Tom Marriott, caught sight of the other two dancing together and was watching Paul's graceful movements, quite unaware that she was doing so, and she didn't know that Marriott had been speaking to her.

'I'm sorry,' she apologized, as her attention came back to him. 'I wasn't listening.'

'Purposefully or otherwise?' he questioned grimly. 'I said that I've heard of your reputation where kissing is concerned.

I don't intend cutting out the love scenes in your part. You'd better understand that from the beginning.'

Kerry swallowed hard and the hobgoblin that had been at the back of her mind somewhere ever since she first accepted the part of Metani now came to the front of her consciousness and gibbered at her as she considered the prospect. Her mood was more one of apprehension, rather than the urge to flare up. It was too easy to imagine being kissed by Paul. He would have that glinting look in his eyes and there would be an insidious caress in his hold of her. She still remembered too well the magnetic thrill the touch of his hand had given her when he had very forcibly held it beneath his on the wheel of the car.

'Well?' said Tom Marriott, waiting for her answer.

'No . . . no, I suppose you can't cut them out,' she said slowly, then became aware that he was laughing at her.

'It won't be too bad,' he said jokingly. 'Paul does it rather well, you know.' Kerry refused to look up and he added in a musing tone, 'You're a funny girl, Kerry. I know hundreds of would-be actresses and quite a few established ones, who would give their eyes to be in a film with Paul, yet you're almost on the point of refusing the part because of a few love scenes.'

She looked up then and a smile trembled on her lips. The vague idea of giving up the part died as she berated herself for being a coward.

'I really will do my best—and I'll try not to give Paul a black eye when he kisses me,' she added.

'Who said you would get a chance to give me a black eye?' Paul's voice inquired, as the music stopped, and she turned quickly to find him right behind her, with Valma at his side.

They went off the floor together and sat down at their table. Kerry finished off her champagne. She found it was beginning to give her a queer, bubbling excitement. She was also beginning to feel warm, but wouldn't take off the jacket.

A short while later Tom Marriott was asking Valma to dance, and the couple took to the floor again.

Kerry watched them go and wished they hadn't. Even though she evaded looking at him, she could feel Paul's eyes on her. To make matters worse, the lace jacket was stifling her, mainly the fault of the tight, high neck, and she tugged at it gently.

'Why don't you take it off?' Paul asked. He saw her hesitation and his smile grew teasing. 'I believe you're afraid.'

The reckless excitement the champagne had given her overruled her caution. 'What of?' she said airily.

'Me.' His reply was succinct and challenging. The dancing light was back in his eyes.

'Certainly not!' she retorted.

'Then take it off.' He leaned back in his chair, watching the play of colour on her face. 'You'll have to get used to a lot more than that, you little idiot.'

Kerry was caught in a cleft stick. She definitely didn't want to take the jacket off, but to keep it on would be to admit her fear of the expression she knew would come to his eyes. It was more than she could stand, though, to be a self-confessed coward.

Delaying the actual moment, she first unpinned the spray of orchids and laid them on the table, then her fingers went to the fastening of the little jacket and drew it off.

Paul nodded, his eyes appreciatively on the slim shoulders. 'Very nice.' His eyes said a lot more, those too expressive black eyes, and she blushed vividly as she bent her head to pin on the orchid spray again.

'You're not helping matters looking at me like that,' she said, using the flowers as an excuse to keep her head bent and taking a long time to twitch them into place.

'Why shouldn't I look at you?' he retorted, deliberately misunderstanding her. 'You're very pleasant to look at.'

'I didn't mean that.' She was getting confused and not quite sure of what she was saying. 'It was the way you were looking.'

She had a vague idea that was something she shouldn't have said. It left the matter open for him to make too many telling retorts, which he wouldn't lose the opportunity of grasping. Silence would be far the safest defence.

He looked at her through half closed eyes, but she could see, in the one brief glance she gave him, that those devil glints were still there, dancing blackly, and the amused smile was still turning his lips.

'What way?' he asked, and his voice was very soft. Somehow the look in his eyes was reflected in it.

She had the feeling he was playing with her, like a cat with a mouse, but she was quite helpless.

'Well, as if . . . if . . .' She stumbled into silence, painfully conscious that she was one huge blush all over and that the parts of her skin that were exposed would all be flying a betraying red banner. Why must she be making such a point of the matter, when he so obviously wanted her to? It would be much better just to drop it, to ignore the look in his eyes and not, in her inexperience, call forth any of the kind of remarks she could not counter. What she could have said was that he looked at her as if . . .

She couldn't put it into words, even in her own mind, but she knew exactly what she meant. And so did Paul. She could see it in the lazy amusement in his expression.

'Anyway, you know just what I mean,' she finished defiantly.

Paul looked exaggeratedly innocent. 'But I don't.'

Kerry scowled at him, but a grin was beginning to twitch her lips. 'Oh yes, you do, and don't look so innocent. It doesn't suit you, and your reputation doesn't make you out as being very innocent.'

'You little devil,' he said softly.

Kerry chuckled. Her misgivings had gone. 'I would like some more champagne,' she requested.

'Well, you don't get any,' he assured her. 'One glass is quite enough for the first time and I think even that one is going to your head slightly. I don't want to have to confront your father with a tipsy Miss Derwin in my arms.'

'Don't you?' Kerry retorted cheekily. 'The way you were looking at me a moment ago I thought you wanted to get me in your clutches.'

One brow went up quizzically. 'Aren't you afraid of being in my clutches, with my reputation?' he asked her.

She shrugged. 'Oh,' with a little toss of her head, 'I can manage you,' she said airily.

A smile twitched at Paul's lips. 'I might remind you that there's still the drive home, so don't pile up too much retaliation.'

Kerry shrugged with mocking carelessness. 'Oh, I'll think about that later. At the moment I would like to dance.' She felt quite safe in the crowded hotel ballroom and didn't think any further ahead or behind, to the time she had been dancing with him before. The sense of power she had felt earlier and the champagne were a heady combination.

When they danced, Kerry could feel the warmth of that insidiously caressing hand on her back, through the thin material of her dress and every now and again his fingers would lightly touch the bare skin above the band of tiny white feathers, sending the usual shivering excitement through her as his magnetism and nearness affected her. She was held so tightly against him she could feel his heart beating and knew he must feel her young breasts crushed against him. There was no doubt at all this time that his lips touched her cheek. It was not a ghostly touch and she attempted to push him away with one hand on his shoulder.

'Paul!' she protested.

'I thought you said you could handle me,' he sent back mockingly.

Kerry swallowed painfully. She knew only too well now that she shouldn't have crossed swords with him. This was different from sparring with Rick or Kel. He was too much the hunter and she the quarry. Now she sensed a trap hidden somewhere and wanted to run.

After this evening she would avoid him, refuse to see him again. It should be fairly easy if she whipped up her old scorn and dislike. Soon the film company would leave Rylston and she wouldn't see him any more.

Then she remembered Metani and knew she couldn't go on with the part. She didn't know quite what it was she feared, but she knew quite clearly now that, in spite of her bantering words, she couldn't bear the thought of those sensuous and almost cruel lips on hers. The Kerry Derwin of the fancy dress ball was awake again, defensive and wary. She sensed the marauding male behind his half joking words.

'I can't go on with it,' she said suddenly through stiff lips.

Paul held her away slightly to look down into her face. The mockery and rapier-swift devils in his eyes had gone. He was serious, the Paul Devron who had asked for her friendship on the moors.

'What can't you go on with, Kerry?' he asked quietly, and his hold had loosened until it was only lightly that he held her.

'The part of Metani,' she answered breathlessly and, even though his hold had relaxed, she still felt as if he held her prisoner. 'I can't do it! I can't. Really I can't!'

He swung her round in a graceful curve that drew them nearer the great french windows that opened on to the terraced gardens.

'Why can't you, Kerry?' His voice was quiet and reassuring, as if he spoke to a child. He read his answer in her face and his own hardened.

'I don't know whether you're a prude, shy, a coward or just a plain cold little fish,' he said at last very quietly. 'However, we shall soon find out,' and before she realized his intention he swung her through the open windows and out into the soft darkness of the gardens.

He drew her down the steps and out of sight of those inside, his hold on her wrist firm and ruthless when she would have struggled with him.

Kerry knew what to expect the moment they left the ballroom. She knew also that it was impossible to fight him, but still she struggled against his irresistible strength. His fingers were like steel on her wrist.

He stopped and turned her to face him. With a deft, experienced ease, one hand went round her waist. The other hand fastened into the hair at the back of her head and forced it up. She had a brief glimpse of his dark, vivid face bent towards her in the moonlight, then his lips touched hers. It was a teasing, provocative kiss, only gently brushing her lips, but hot and trembling, she tried to draw away. His hand kept her head still and gradually the pressure on her lips increased. The arm around her waist tightened, in spite of her protesting stiffness.

He lifted his head momentarily. 'Don't be such a little idiot, Kerry,' he whispered.

His lips had a cool warmth against hers. They were not passionate and frightening. Rather they were provocative, exciting.

Was she being a fool? Kerry wondered suddenly. She forced herself to let the taut, stiff lines of her body relax and felt his arms hold her closer yet. The stiff lips softened under his but still didn't respond. Yet she found it was different when she didn't fight. There was an unexpected delight and enchantment and then she found she didn't have to force herself to relax. She liked the feel of his lips and when he took his hand away from the back of her head she didn't move away.

Paul lifted his head again and held her slightly away from him. He looked down into her face and his smile had no triumph or mockery.

'Well?' His voice and eyes were teasing. 'It wasn't so bad, was it?'

'No,' she admitted in a very small voice.

He held her against him and his fingers gently twined in her vivid hair.

'Perhaps it was even a little pleasant,' he suggested persuasively.

'Yes.' Kerry made the admission in the same very small voice, from the vicinity of his shoulder.

'Then do you think you could take the part of Metani now?'

'Yes.' The fear was gone now. There was nothing to stop her taking the part. She had been kissed by Paul Devron and found it was not so frightening as she had expected. She even recognized the truth of her admission that it was pleasant. And now that it was all over she felt ashamed of her childish fear.

'Thank you for being so patient with me, Paul,' she said quietly, and somehow felt much older. She had grown a little the night of the fancy dress dance. Tonight she had grown still more. If she had met Barbie at that moment, she would have realized instantly the gulf between them that had not been evident such a few short weeks ago.

'You're sure you've got over your fear now?' His voice was still teasing and when she nodded he added: 'Then prove it.'

She knew what he meant, but her shyness kept her motionless until he drew her close to him again. She felt the strength of his arms, but this time she wasn't afraid. There was a thrilling delight in knowing herself a prisoner to the strength of the man.

'I can see I shall have to give you a little private tuition before we start rehearsing before all the others,' he said softly, and laughed as she blushed vividly. 'What a shy child you are! You'll have to learn not to do that as well—unless you want me to keep on kissing you.' There was a trace of the old lilting devil-may-care in his voice. 'Don't you know that a blush comes out like a dirty face on the screen? We would have to keep on rehearsing until you didn't blush.'

'I didn't know,' she whispered. 'But how am I going to stop it?'

'You'll be surprised how soon you'll get used to it,' he said reassuringly. 'Not that I would mind at all. You're very pleasant to kiss. Didn't you know?' Kerry shook her head and he went on: 'Now do as I told you.'

Very shyly, she raised her arms and linked them around his neck. Her lips were soft and tremulous when he kissed her and timidly responsive.

'That's enough for the first lesson,' he said, and released her, except for one hand beneath her elbow. 'I think we'd better go in now. Tom has a spare copy of the script up in his room. I'll ask him to get it so that you can take it home with you tonight, my little Metani.'

They went in together and started dancing as if there had been no interruption, and Kerry was happy again. He still held her closely and they still sparred, but now her fear had gone from her. Before she had feared him to kiss her. Now he had done so and she had found she liked it. She could spar with him now, careless of retribution on the journey home.

What matter if they crossed swords and he won? She found the lot of the defeated unusually sweet.

CHAPTER FIVE

KERRY came into The House one afternoon waving a large envelope excitedly.

'I've got it!' she called out, and both her father and Mallie came out of their respective cubbyholes to see just what had made her so excited. They converged in the hallway where Kerry was standing still waving her prize.

'What is it that you've so dramatically got?' her father inquired.

Kerry looked a little surprised, as if they should know instinctively what she was talking about.

'Why, the part of Metani, of course,' she said. 'The tests were successful and I have to start on some coaching work on Monday.'

'Good work!' Richard Derwin was almost as excited as she was. Mallie was speechless.

'This should call for a celebration of some sort,' Kerry's father announced.

'I'll go and put the kettle on,' Mallie rejoined promptly, and padded off down the corridor to the kitchen.

'Not a very exciting beverage, but we'll drink to your future in a cup of tea, Kerry,' Richard Derwin said with his roguish chuckle. He tweaked her hair affectionately as they followed Mallie. 'It seems rather startling to think of my wild and harum-scarum daughter becoming a film star.'

Kerry wrinkled her nose. 'Not a star,' she corrected him whimsically. 'Just a little bit of comet dust. It's funny,' she added reflectively. 'At the beginning I wasn't really too interested when Mr. Marriott first asked me. I'd never really thought of anything like that, but now I really do want to play the part of Metani.'

Her father shot her a sly sideways glance as they entered the kitchen. 'What I would like to see is the first time they try to get you in a love scene.'

Mallie stopped rattling cups and listened for Kerry's answer. Kerry, however, rather surprised them by laughing ruefully.

'I deserved that after all I've said on the subject!'

The familiar absent look crossed her father's face. 'I had a heroine like you once,' he remarked, à propos of nothing.

Kerry leaned her chin on her hands. 'Oh,' she said interested. 'What happened to her?'

He made a vague gesture. 'I think she ended up by getting married and having about ten children.'

His daughter grimaced. 'No, thank you,' she said very decidedly. 'I have no intention of getting married and less still of having ten children.'

'Oh well,' Richard Derwin said, with a return to his vague manner. 'We'll see.'

It was a merry little tea party, but Kerry wished that Rick was there. Kelvin too. But Rick was back at college and Kelvin had gone to stay with some relations in Cornwall for a short period of further training. A cousin there owned stables about six times as big as the Treveryl ones. She hadn't seen Barbie either for a couple of weeks. She began to feel somehow as if the old and familiar things were growing away from her. Was there even a subtle difference in her father's and Mallie's manner?

* * *

During the weeks that followed, Kerry found her new work becoming daily more engrossing. She missed Rick and Kelvin at first, but there was so much happening that, guilty as she felt about it, they began to fade into the background.

During the time she was being intensively coached in her part, she saw little of Paul. On the brief instances she did see him he looked tired and she knew that he was working exceedingly hard. It somehow gave her a little worried feeling, although she couldn't understand why it should.

The coach was staying in the same hotel as Paul, like a lot of other film people. Sometimes she found herself hoping for a glimpse of the man she had once professed to scorn. There were a few others girls attending the coach, but she never really made friends with them, mainly through their fault. Kerry was not standoffish, although she could be decidedly cantankerous and elusive if she didn't like anyone. They knew that she had a star part waiting for her and that seemed to set her aside from them.

One afternoon as she had just finished her lesson and was leaving the hotel, an excited voice hailed her.

'Kerry!'

She recognized Barbie's voice and turned

eagerly. It was weeks since she had seen the other girl and she watched the short, plumpish figure crossing the road to her with smiling eyes.

'Hallo, Barbie.'

'Oh, Kerry!' Barbie said breathlessly. 'Is it true that you're going to act with Paul Devron?' Her eyes were big and round.

'Yes,' Kerry answered, somewhat cautiously. After all she had said to Barbie on the subject of Paul Devron, she expected to receive some retaliatory teasing.

It didn't occur to Barbie, however. She let out a sigh of pure envy. 'To act with Paul Devron! You of all people.' She grasped Kerry's arm. 'What's he like? Did he insist on carrying out the terms of that raffle?'

Kerry had begun to smile as Barbie fired questions at her, but at the last she involuntarily flushed and the younger girl read it quite correctly.

'Oh, Kerry!' Her eyes were frankly envious. 'What was it like?'

Kerry moved uncomfortably. It was something she didn't care to discuss even with Barbie.

'It was quite pleasant,' she said at last,

with a studied indifference.

'Quite pleasant!' Barbie's voice rose on a squeal of indignation. 'Quite pleasant! What a tame way to describe it!'

Kerry frowned thoughtfully. Now that she really came to think of it, it had been rather a tame kiss. It hadn't occurred to her at the time, but somehow it didn't seem quite the way he kissed on the screen. Then she shrugged it off. Probably pure imagination, of course. How could kisses be different, except of course that some kisses were nicer than others. Paul's were far more pleasant than Frank Connors' would have been.

'What's the film about?' Barbie was firing questions again. 'What's your part like?'

Kerry hesitated. Again she sensed the gulf. Barbie seemed to her now a child, but she knew she would not have been aware of it a few short weeks ago.

She gestured towards a teashop. 'Let's go in here and have some tea. I'll tell you about it there.'

Kerry ordered tea and cakes with an assurance she subconsciously realized she wouldn't have had a few weeks ago and when they arrived she pushed the cakes over towards Barbie, as if offering a child the creamiest of them. Nothing loth, Barbie took one bursting with cream and started munching happily. She seemed to have reached a new acceptance of Kerry and was quite unselfconscious again.

'Now what about the film?' she asked.

'It's called *Moorland Duel.*' Kerry broke off and leaned her chin on her hands for a thoughtful moment, remembering back to the night Paul had first kissed her. He had kissed her again when he drove her home, expertly and passionlessly. She had finally gone to bed that night tired and completely happy.

Then she had read the script. Her eyes had widened at some of the things Metani was supposed to say—and do. She had an intense feeling of doubt the first time she read through the love scenes, but it had passed and she had settled down contentedly to her lessons. Acting the part of Metani didn't have to start for a while and in any case she still believed that Paul wouldn't kiss her any differently, but by some magic of the screen, they would come out as the searing embraces he was famous for.

'Go on,' Barbie said impatiently, and

Kerry started back to the present.

'The story is about a noblewoman, Lady Frances Brandon—that's Valma,' she added, 'who falls in love with the leader of a tribe of Spanish gypsies who had been brought over to dance in some festivities and subsequently stayed in England. Paul of course plays the gypsy leader.'

Barbie's eyes grew dreamy. 'I can imagine him in the part,' she said, and then, expecting a scathing comment on her daydreaming, added hastily: 'Anyway, go on.'

Kerry hadn't been going to make the expected comment. She had changed a lot from the old Kerry who'd been so intolerant of her friend's adolescent hero-worship.

'When the story begins,' she said, 'the gypsy leader is just being told about a witch girl, Metani, who's supposed to live on some secret island out in the bog, that only she knows how to reach.'

'Who plays Metani?' Barbie asked, and looked intrigued when the other girl indicated herself.

'Metani leaves the secret island one day,' Kerry continued, 'and is captured by the gypsies and forced to marry their chieftain when he falls in love with her. All this happened a few hundred years ago, so they could get away with things like that,' she explained, and Barbie nodded, drinking it in. 'The witch girl isn't really unwilling, because she claims that further in the past, way back in Roman times, the gypsy and she had been lovers before. Just after the marriage, however, the gypsy chief catches sight of the Lady Frances and just falls flat for her, forgetting all about Metani. He leaves her and follows the Lady Frances, who although she is attracted to him despises him for his low birth. Metani in turn follows him and tries to persuade him to come back to her, telling him about their life in Roman times. That's when there's a flashback in the film, showing it. He still leaves her and goes to the Lady Frances, who finally confesses to being in love with him, but the witch girl goes back to her secret island and is supposed to use witchcraft to try to get him back. She succeeds and he leaves Lady Frances. Altogether it's a pretty stupid film,' she added.

'It sounds good,' Barbie objected. 'Go on. Who gets him in the end?'

Kerry looked surprised. 'The witch girl,

of course, I thought I told you. It ends with Lady Frances standing at the door of her great house, gazing into the distance.'

'Oh!' It looked as if Barbie didn't like the fade-out scene, but she quickly brightened. 'I'm glad you get him in the end.'

Kerry threw her a quizzical glance and didn't comment. Shortly afterwards she left and collecting Smoky from the Treveryl stables, started the homeward journey.

She was very thoughtful as she rode and there was a pensive frown in her eyes. The difference between Barbie and herself was now too pronounced to be ignored any longer. Did growing up mean losing your friends? Not always, though. There were those who grew up with you, but there had always been two years' difference between Barbie and herself. It hadn't seemed noticeable in the past. It was now.

But if she had lost one friend, she had gained others. There were Tom Marriott and Valma. And Paul.

As if the thought of him had conjured him up, she heard his voice. Turning, she saw him cantering slowly towards her on a large black stallion that she recognized as coming from the Treveryl stables. It was the horse he rode in the film. He was wearing not the gypsy dress, though, but khaki riding breeches and a white silk shirt that was open at the neck to show darkly tanned skin. His black hair was ruffled by the wind, instead of lying sleekly flat, as it usually did. Although he looked superbly attractive and somehow younger, she could see he was very tired.

'Hallo, Kerry,' he said, and smiled in greeting.

'Hallo, Paul,' she returned. 'You look tired.' She hadn't thought she could know so much pleasure in unexpectedly meeting someone. It was true, though. The world had become strangely brighter and her appreciation of it had increased. Even so, she made her tone as normal as possible.

'I'm tired,' he said. 'They're shooting scenes this afternoon where I'm not wanted, so I went on strike.'

Kerry looked up at him a little anxiously as he passed a hand somewhat wearily across his eyes. He was different from the usual self-assured Paul Devron and she felt an unfamiliar emotion stirring inside her.

'Where are you going now?' she asked.

'Nowhere in particular. Just riding.' He glanced at her with an unconsciously pleading smile. 'Do you have to go straight home, Kerry, or will you come with me?'

Kerry sensed his need of her and it seemed quite natural that she should want to help him.

'Of course I'll come,' she said instantly. 'I'd better. You might go wandering into a bog.'

He turned to look at her again and a hint of the old teasing was in his eyes. 'Would you care if I did?'

'Of course I would.' She dropped her eyes and sought to bring a facetious note into the conversation. 'Besides, what would all your fans say?'

'They would transfer their attention to someone else,' he retorted with a touch of the cynicism he rarely showed with her. 'The public is a fickle animal, Kerry.'

'Oh, well, I suppose for the sake of your career, I shall have to see that you stay in the safe parts of the moors,' she rejoined with studied casualness.

For a moment the old teasing broke through and she thought he was going to make some blush-provoking comment on her last remark, but he merely smiled and didn't say anything.

It was still early afternoon and although they rode slowly Kerry knew where they were going; a place to which there was no trail. It didn't occur to her as being strange that, when she had never taken even Rick or Kelvin there, she should be taking Paul.

After a while she turned off the faintly defined trail they had been following and plunged into wild-looking country. When at length she stopped it was on top of a low hill and below them dreamed a tiny valley where a miniature stream tinkled with a single great tree overhanging its banks.

She turned to Paul with a smile. 'Like it?'

He looked round appreciatively, at the little valley that belonged in a fairytale, and nodded.

'It's lovely, Kerry. These moors of yours have some unexpected little beauty spots.'

'The whole moors are lovely,' she replied. 'Even the dangerous parts, the bogs with the mists rising from them at night, have a weird kind of beauty.'

He looked at her sideways. She was a creature of the moors. She would bring Metani to life, the wild witch girl of the moors.

They rode down into the valley and dismounted. It was warm with a drowsy quietness and the horses cropped the long grass contentedly, as their riders lounged in it. Kerry plucked a long strand of grass and sat pulling it through her fingers. Paul, leaning against the great tree trunk, watched her with the same drowsy quiet contentedness of the valley.

As if in answer to some unspoken request, she turned suddenly and looked at him.

He held out his hand. 'Come here.'

Without hesitation she moved over to his side, leaning against the tree. There was not much room to spare and she could feel his warm, strong body close to hers, but this afternoon she didn't have the instinctive desire to escape. He looked so tired and yet at the same time so contented she had an absurd and maternal desire to put an arm around him and draw his head down on her shoulder. It was absurd, she knew, to feel like that about Paul Devron, yet it seemed so natural at this moment—so natural that she did so.

He gave her a brief startled glance, then a wholly satisfied smile. 'You're an unexpected and wonderful little person, Kerry Derwin,' he murmured.

Kerry smiled slightly. 'Am I?'

'Yes. You and your little valley.' He

paused and then, after a moment, added: 'I wish you could see my little cabin up in the Rockies, Kerry. It's isolated by the side of a deep blue lake and surrounded by snow-capped mountains. The only way to get there is by plane. I always escape up there between films.'

'Is Paul Devron your real name?' she asked curiously.

Paul moved his head slowly. 'Not quite. It's Paul de Veronil. My mother was English, my father French-Canadian. I was born in the Rockies.'

'Tell me about your home,' she urged softly.

'It was a little ranch. My mother was a cripple. My father had died when I was small, and I don't remember much about him. There were a couple of ranch hands there as well. We were all pretty happy on the ranch, though. There wasn't much money, but what there was seemed adequate.

'My mother died just after I left school. I sold the ranch and after that, I just drifted for a while. Then I came to Hollywood.'

He didn't need to go any further. Kerry, although professing a complete disinterest in the subject, had heard of his meteoric rise to stardom through Barbie. One film had made him overnight. They called him the second Valentino. Some critics said that the first film was just a fluke, that his second would be a flop. Then the second came and the enchantment was still there. And the third, the fourth... One film after another, and all the while his popularity increased. Also, it wasn't only the women who liked him. Apart from that other more unusual gift he had, he was a superb actor. It was strange to think of him coming from the quiet peaks of the Rockies to the bright lights of Hollywood.

'Didn't you find it strange after the Rockies?' she asked.

Again he smiled, this time without looking up. 'It was strange, at first. It's brittle and artificial, the cameras and the noise and the sets, but I don't think I could ever leave it now. It gets into your blood, Kerry.'

Again he became quiet and this time he didn't speak again. After a moment she looked down and saw that his eyes had closed. His breathing was even and deep. He was fast asleep.

Very gently she eased him down until he lay on the grass and sat with her back against the tree, watching him.

It would have seemed impossible to the Kerry Derwin of a while ago that she could be acting as she was, yet it was something engendered by the calm quietness of the valley. It wouldn't always be like this, she knew, but an endearing side of him had been revealed this afternoon that she knew she would never forget.

She let him sleep for a while, but she knew she would have to awaken him before very long. Mallie would worry if she was long overdue in returning to The House.

Curiously she leaned over him. Her fingers accidentally touched his windblown black hair. It was silky and vibrantly alive. His face in repose was a little lonely. The well-formed but sensual mouth slightly sulky. His eyelashes made darker smudges on his dark skin.

Her eyes left his face, came to rest on his hands. They were slim and long-fingered, but strong as steel. She knew that well. It was the same with his body. Even in sleep it had a look of relaxed power, the slim lithe power of a panther. The simile came to her suddenly, as she remembered the black panther she had once seen asleep at the zoo. It was here too, the dark dancer's grace, the ruthlessness.

The panther also had fascinated her.

But it was getting late. She knew she would have to awaken him. One hand went out to shake his shoulder, then she stopped. Instead she bent over and lightly touched his lips with her own.

Instantly one arm whipped up around her neck, holding her to him. Because he had been startled, his kiss was warmer than usual, but it was still not enough to frighten her.

Still holding her, he opened his eyes and Kerry felt the hot blood rush to her face at their expression. They were no longer drowsy and tired. They were appreciative, dancing with all their old impudence.

'That was a lovely way to awaken me,' he murmured, touching his lips to the hot cheek nearest him. 'Thank you, Kerry darling.'

Kerry wrenched herself away and climbed to her feet. 'It's time we were getting back,' she said primly.

He came to his feet in a single lithe movement, like a coiled spring suddenly released. His eyes still glinted and she realized his former mood was completely dispelled. He was dangerous again, but like the black panther, he still fascinated her.

They went over to their horses and Kerry sprang into Smoky's saddle before he could offer to help her mount, not that she ever needed any help.

They rode away from the valley and after a few minutes Kerry realized that she was in for a bout of the teasing that could bring the hot colour to her cheeks so quickly. She turned the subject off a more personal one and asked him about the dances in the film. She liked to talk about dancing, and in any case it was a safe topic.

'I gather that's about the only thing you approve of in my films,' he answered with an amused twinkle in his eyes.

Kerry shifted her shoulders a little uncomfortably. 'Oh well . . .' she began undecidedly, but he cut across her words with a laugh.

'All right. You needn't go on. I know your opinion of love scenes too well. I'm glad you approve of my dancing anyway.'

'I love dancing.' Her eyes lit up enthusiastically. 'There was one dance, Paul. I even bought the soundtrack record.'

He glanced at her and smiled. 'Which one was it? I'll teach you it if you like.'

Kerry's eyes now sparkled with absolute

delight. 'The Argentine tango in *Pampas Moon*,' she said promptly.

Paul looked blank. Very vividly he could remember the sensualism and passion of that particular dance. Very vividly also he could imagine Miss Derwin's reactions if she found herself in his arms, dancing that tango. It was so characteristic of her that she had been intrigued by the dance and missed everything else.

His eyes danced with absolute amusement as he said: 'So you want to learn that dance, Kerry?'

Kerry nodded eagerly. 'Please.' She reflected for a moment on just who he was and then added with surprising diffidence, 'That's if you really don't mind teaching it to me.'

'Mind?' He threw back his head in quick laughter. 'I wouldn't dare, Kerry my sweet.'

She looked surprised. 'Why?'

The amused dark eyes went over her puzzled face. 'Because you would hit me—very hard,' he said.

Again she gave him a thoroughly puzzled look. 'Why?' she asked for the second time.

The amusement gave way to the leaping black devils she knew so well. 'All right—

but on one condition,' he stipulated. 'You do exactly as I tell you.'

Kerry nodded in instant agreement. 'I promise,' she said, but gave him a wary glance nevertheless. 'So long as you also promise not to improvise.'

'I won't need to,' he replied, and let her puzzle that out for the rest of the journey to The House.

They left their horses with Joddy and went into the house. Mallie appeared from the kitchen, delighted and flustered at the same time seeing who Kerry had brought home with her.

'I'll just make some tea,' she said, and scampered off towards the kitchen.

'We'll be in the dancing room,' Kerry called after her.

'The dancing room?' Paul raised one dark brow inquiringly.

'It used to belong to my mother,' she explained. 'We always called it that. A lot of her old ballet dresses are still there. That's where my evening dress came from,' she added confidentially. 'I often dance up there myself.'

'Then go and put one of them on now,' he ordered jokingly. 'I refuse to teach that tango to a girl wearing riding clothes. It just doesn't fit.'

Kerry knew he was only joking, but the idea appealed to her. 'All right,' she agreed and, surprising him, started to run up the stairs. 'I won't be a moment,' she called out as she saw her father come out of his study.

Richard Derwin regarded the flying figure of his daughter for a moment in silence, then turned to the man. The last Kerry saw of them both they were going into his study, absorbed in each other's conversation, as if she was already forgotten.

Upstairs in the room where her mother's portrait hung upon the wall, Kerry rummaged in the inset wardrobe. Finally she found what she wanted, a costume that had been made for a ballet with a Spanish setting. Quickly she stripped off her riding things and put on the costume. Before going downstairs she went to her own room and fastened on a pair of her own silver dancing shoes.

They must have heard her coming, because the door of her father's study opened again and the two men came out. Her father was grinning widely and she wondered just what they had been talking about.

'I've told Mallie to hold the tea up for a while, until after you've had your dancing lesson,' he said. 'You'll probably need it—after all the exertion, of course,' he added blandly, and went back into his study.

Kerry and Paul were left facing each other. The man's eyes went over her appreciatively.

'Why don't you wear feminine clothes more often, Kerry?' he asked.

She shrugged unconcernedly. 'They're silly and uncomfortable. Besides, I'm more used to riding things or slacks.'

He made no further comment, but followed her up the stairs. When she opened the door into the long room that was lit by the afternoon sunlight, he looked round appreciatively, then crossed to the portrait of the woman that hung on the wall.

'Is this your mother?' he asked softly. 'She's very lovely.'

Kerry came to stand at his side. 'Yes,' she said. 'I never knew her.'

'She's like you, except for the red hair,' he commented.

Kerry read the hidden compliment in his words and flushed slightly as she turned away to find the tango record. Paul had switched on the record player when she turned with it in her hand and as he took the record from her and placed it on the turntable, she saw that the twin black devils of amusement were dancing in his eyes. She began to wonder just what was causing the amusement. Perhaps the dance was hard. She put the thought into words and he shook his head.

'No, it's remarkably simple, Kerry. It's the particular way it's danced, and the music.'

He started the record and then with an incredibly swift movement caught one of her hands and jerked her towards him. Before she had quite realized what had happened she found she was completely off balance and supported entirely by Paul's arms. Even as a gasp of surprise was forced from her lips, he had straightened up and spun round with her in his arms with a peculiar halting, half savage gliding movement. For the first time she became aware of the insidious undercurrent in the music. There was a throbbing beat that shivered through her senses. It whispered of things she didn't understand but that set her nerves to a mad, almost frightened quivering. It spoke of many things, and she didn't want to listen.

She bit her lips and tried to break away. Surprisingly Paul let her go, but not for long. Even as she backed away from him, unconsciously still keeping in time with the music, with another of those ruthless jerking movements he caught her hand and brought her close again. With inescapable ease, his hands gripped her body and swung her over backwards. Almost immediately he straightened up. His right hand held her left rigidly upheld and, as they paused motionless on the beat of the music, with a slow deliberate sensualism, his fingers moved down her bare arm and fastened in the mane of fiery hair at the back of her neck.

Kerry stared at him as if hypnotized and the music came to an end with a final crashing chord.

Paul released her and turned the record off. 'That's enough for now, and anyway it isn't the full version. They've cut a lot out.'

'Have they?' Kerry said in an uncertain voice, and was privately glad that the record had been shortened. She understood now his amusement when she had announced what dance she wanted to learn.

When Paul turned round he was smiling.

'Serves you right,' he said unsympathetically. 'You wanted to dance it. I let you off lightly. There's a lot more.'

'Is there?'

'There is,' he replied, mocking her own tone. 'When do you want your next lesson?' Through half-closed eyes he watched a suspicious red tinge come into her face.

'Oh, it doesn't matter,' she said evasively. 'You're probably rather busy with the film.'

'Not too busy,' he countered unhelpfully.

Kerry gave him a sulky glance for making things so difficult. She didn't want to have to admit that she found the dance too disturbing to go on with, yet it was a different feeling from when he had kissed her. This gave the sensation of something waiting just beyond the threshold of restraint.

'Of course,' he commented, and she heard a faintly mocking tinge in his voice. 'The truth is you're afraid.'

Her head came up defiantly. 'Certainly not!' she retorted.

'Really?'

She looked away and refused to continue discussion of the subject. 'I feel like some tea now.'

'Coward!' he jeered, but she refused to rise. Determinedly, she led the way out of the room.

CHAPTER SIX

AFTER the dance incident, Kerry saw no more of the man who so persistently occupied her thoughts, until the day she was at last summoned to appear on the set of *Moorland Duel*.

At the end of one of her coaching lessons she turned to see Tom Marriott watching her from the doorway.

He came forward into the room with an encouraging smile. 'Quite good, Kerry.'

She blushed shyly. 'Thank you.'

'Read up your lines for the Roman scene over the week-end,' he instructed. 'Paul will pick you up on Monday morning. We're ready to begin shooting.'

'Oh!' Kerry swallowed hard. It was all she could say at the moment. It had come at last, then.

He smiled reassuringly at her panic-stricken look. 'Don't worry. You'll be all right.'

Kerry swallowed again. She had just remembered that the Roman flashback involved a love scene. Why did they have to pick something like that to start on?

Very dutifully, though, she went home and made sure that she thoroughly knew her lines. She wandered about the house restlessly, alternately having fits of excitement or fright. Her father and Mallie took it in turns to reassure her when she stated miserably that she wouldn't remember a word, couldn't act and felt cold at the very thought.

Monday arrived quicker than she had thought days could fly. By that time she was a bundle of nerves and shivering trepidation. On Monday also arrived Paul Devron, in the familiar black car.

'Oh, Paul, I'm scared! I feel sick!' Kerry told him.

'Nonsense,' he assured her. 'You'll be all right.'

Richard Derwin appeared at the top of the stairs and came down to them. He smiled in greeting at the actor and then glanced over at his daughter.

'Of course you'll be all right. You've just got an attack of nerves.' He glanced again at Paul. 'Have you time for some tea before you go? Sorry I can't offer you a drink.'

'Thanks, but I think we'd better go,' Devron replied, 'or this child will fold up and go into a coma.' He gave Kerry's wrist a gentle shake and made his tone deliberately jeering. 'Come on, brace up, you little coward. You always worry about things beforehand, then find they're not so bad after all.'

She knew he was referring to the time he had kissed her and his tone had the desired effect of pulling her together. Her eyes sparkled with the familiar battle light, and he laughed.

'That's better.'

As they turned towards the door, Mallie called out: 'Good luck, Miss Kerry,' and Richard Derwin added his own good wishes.

In the black car that was taking her away from The House and towards the unfamiliar territory of her new career, Kerry nervously smoothed the material of her navy blue slacks with hands she tried to stop trembling, and wondered again if she was wearing the correct clothes. It had taken her some time to decide, although there hadn't really been much choice.

There were the two dresses, faded and too small, her riding clothes or a blouse and slacks. She had chosen the latter and looked neat and attractive, but was quite unaware of it, and in her present mood would probably have been uncaring even if she had noticed.

'Cheer up, Kerry,' Paul said whimsically at her side. 'You're not going to your execution, you know, even if there does happen to be a love scene ahead of you.'

A ghost of her gamin grin peeped out for a moment. 'That doesn't scare me anymore.'

'Don't you believe it,' he retorted darkly. 'You've a lot to learn yet.' Kerry caught his glance and burst out laughing and he added approvingly: 'That's better.'

Before her nervousness and fright could come back, he started to sing an absurd little song that had been popular a few months ago and after a moment Kerry joined in. When the camp came in sight, however, she abruptly became silent again, twisting her hands together in her lap.

Paul reached out and took one as he stopped the car. 'Relax, Kerry.' He gave it a reassuring pressure, then dropped it and came quickly round to her side of the car to open the door.

She gave herself a quick mental talking to and slid out of the car, planting her feet firmly on the ground with her chin squared pugnaciously. Paul recognized her look and laughed.

'Don't go quarrelling with everybody just because you feel afraid. If you do, I'll either spank you or kiss you.'

She scowled at him, then reluctant laughter came to her eyes and spread across her face. 'I'd rather you kissed me,' she said impishly. 'I'm sure I'd like that better.'

'Oh, would you?' he retorted. 'I'll ask you which you prefer again one day.'

Kerry read a double meaning there somewhere and remembered her uneasy suspicion that the rather tame kiss he had given her was nothing like the love scenes in some of his films.

Tom and Valma came over to them as she was considering asking Paul to explain what he meant by his last remark.

'Stop trembling, child,' Valma joked, smiling cheerfully. 'We'll only be rehearsing today.'

Kerry gulped and swallowed hard. 'I . . .' she began, and could get no further.

Her head retrogressed rapidly to the woolly state it had been in at the beginning of the drive. Even her knees felt weak and she had a shameful vision of herself collapsing at their feet and being ignominiously sent home again.

'You'll soon snap out of it,' Tom said briskly. 'We'll get to the set now.'

They crossed to where the tents were erected. The last time she had been down there, on the memorable occasion when Valma had nearly walked into the clinging mud of the morass, they had just been in the process of being erected, ancient history being reborn out of confused but somehow orderly chaos. Crowds of extras stood around now, but none of them were in costume.

They crossed to the largest tent and there Tom Marriott stopped. 'We'll take the interior scene,' he said thoughtfully, and motioned them in.

Kerry entered interestedly, forgetting her shyness for the moment. One wall of the tent was entirely missing. That would be for the cameras, she decided. The tent was furnished with amazing luxury for a military establishment, but she remembered that it was supposed to belong to a Roman patrician. Off to one side a table was spread with maps, supposedly of campaigns. It was like entering another world. Nothing bore the least resemblance to the twentieth century—if one looked away from the missing fourth wall of the tent.

Paul crossed to sit behind the desk and Kerry felt quite involuntary amazement creep over her. He wore no costume, his clothes were modern twentieth century trousers and white silk shirt—yet somehow he had altered. He wasn't Paul Devron. His face had hardened; the arrogance had increased. He was Marius, a Roman patrician. His very look made her feel the unwilling captive she was supposed to be, in spite of her own twentieth century clothes.

Marriott nodded and quite naturally she found herself shrinking back and clutching the material of the tent.

Paul laid his hands on the desk and very slowly he rose. All the time his eyes never left her. They swept over her slim, taut figure with an insolent appreciation that made her tremble inwardly and set her nerves to fearful protest. Never before had he looked at her like that. But this was not

Paul, she reminded herself quickly. This was a Roman officer. Whatever dress he wore, this man was a Roman. Behind him was the shadow of the legions—masters of the world, cruel, arrogant, taking what they wanted. And he wanted Metani—or rather Metani's ancestor Layla.

'So!' he said softly. 'The Iceni send women to fight us. Are the men then too afraid to come out of hiding?'

Kerry stiffened and drew herself upright. It was strange, she thought, how easily she could identify herself with this girl in the past.

'Your legions are not destroyed by shadows. You know well where the men are. We women chose to follow our Queen, to avenge the insult to the royal house.' Her words were proud and struck with a bitter intensity. Her identity was sinking almost indistinguishably into that of Metani's ancestor. It was the sort of reply she herself would have made in the circumstances.

Paul came round the desk and stood leaning against it, looking across at her.

'Come here,' he said, still with that dangerously soft note in his voice. When she remained unmoving, he added, still softly, but with a note of authority, 'It will be easy for me to use force. Come here.'

Very slowly she took a few faltering steps nearer. Yet her voice was still proud and firm when she spoke.

'What are you going to do with me?'

'A short while ago you tried to kill me. I shouldn't feel too kindly disposed towards you.'

Her lips curled. 'It was not my fault that I did not succeed.'

'True,' he acknowledged mockingly. 'A fact I am singularly glad of. This proves to be far more entertaining. As a warrior you were dangerous—but as a woman it is possible you are far more so.'

With deliberate slowness he straightened up off the desk and came towards her. Step by step, she backed from him until his voice stopped her.

'Behind you is the camp. Would you go to my men rather than to me?'

She flung her head up defiantly. 'Rather would I go to death!' Her quick leap took her to a small table where a dagger lay and it was raised to bury itself in her heart when his hand wrenched it from her. The knife slipped to the floor and with a little sob she found herself swept high into arms whose strength couldn't be denied. Kerry was totally submerged. It was Layla who struggled in the arms of the Roman as he crossed to the heavy curtains that led into another part of the tent and swept them aside with his shoulder. She was quite unaware of Tom Marriott and the rest of the spellbound audience shifting quietly to a position where they could look into the second half of the tent.

Here a large divan piled with cushions occupied the main part of the tent and Kerry was lowered into them with a gentleness that did not disguise quite unmistakable purpose. Paul sat down beside her and leaned towards her. For one moment she saw his face bent over hers, dark and smiling now, and the dancing black devils in his eyes. His hands gripped her shoulders, pressing her deeper into the cushions, then his mouth came down on hers. Questing lips parted hers with a passionate intensity she couldn't move her head to resist. Shock ran through her startled nerves in trembling waves.

Desperate hands tried to push him away, but his hold was quite ruthless and she was acutely conscious of every line of his body against hers. A strange languor shivered through her and a sense of heady excitement that was different altogether from that she had felt when he had kissed her in the gardens. It was a feeling that robbed her limbs of all strength of power to resist.

When he lifted his head, she looked at him uncomprehendingly for a moment, then slowly realization and fury spread across her face.

'How dare you kiss me like that!' raged Miss Derwin, no longer submerged. Her hand went up to strike his face, but one of his own caught and foiled its warlike intentions. 'How dare you!' she spluttered indignantly.

Paul looked down at her with a smile. 'I told you you had a lot to learn,' he said unrepentantly.

Kerry was about to retort when Marriott and Valma reached them.

'Now what's the matter?' the director snapped impatiently.

Kerry took the opportunity to slip out of Paul's reach and stand up. 'He shouldn't have kissed me like that,' she muttered sulkily, by way of explanation of her unscripted reactions.

Marriott looked blank. 'Why not? You knew there were to be love scenes in your part.'

Kerry threw him an upward, sulky look and nodded.

'Then what's all . . .' he began, when Valma cut across his words.

'Leave me alone with Kerry for a moment,' she requested. 'All of you. Yes, you too, Paul.'

Reluctantly they went and then Valma sat down on the divan and motioned Kerry to take a seat at her side. Neither spoke for a moment, then Kerry moved mutinously.

'Paul's kissed you before, hasn't he?' Valma asked at last, very softly.

Kerry nodded again. 'Yes, he has,' she admitted.

'But not like that?' Valma pursued determinedly, and again the bright head nodded. 'I'm going to ask you a question which I want you to answer absolutely truthfully,' she added. 'Will you?'

Kerry gave her a wary look. 'All right,' she murmured.

'Did you really dislike Paul kissing you like that?'

Kerry's head shot up. Her mouth framed an instant and indignant 'yes', but Valma shook her head and smiled slightly.

'Remember, I said an absolutely truthful

answer, Kerry. Think about it a moment.'

Kerry bit her lips and her eyes fell. Her shoulders moved uneasily.

'No,' she said mutinously.

Valma's smile grew. 'Then what was all the fuss about?'

'It made me feel horrible.'

'Horrible?'

Kerry flashed her a brief upward glance and then away again. 'Sort of trembling and weak,' she muttered ungraciously.

Very firmly the actress took hold of her shoulders and turned her to face her. She looked into the young face for long moments and her smile died.

'You could have been acting opposite somebody you didn't like at all,' Valma told her firmly. 'It could have happened like that, you know. Sometimes I've had to play against actors who absolutely made me prickle and I had to pretend to be in love with them. Then there have been those that arouse just plain boredom or indifference. When you're tied down to a contract you can't do anything about it.'

'Paul made sure I was tied down to a contract before he kissed me like he did,' Kerry flashed back.

'If he did, I rather admire him for it,'

Valma retorted with a quick laugh. 'Perhaps he wanted you to play the part of Metani and was making sure you didn't take fright and refuse.'

She wondered whether she had gone too far, but strangely the old gamin grin broke over Kerry's face.

'The wretch,' she said softly.

Now that she allowed herself to be truthful she realized it had been surprisingly pleasant. It had been mainly indignation against herself that had caused her outcry. She hadn't liked to find the old Kerry Derwin so changed.

Valma rose to her feet and her smile hid triumph. 'Good. I take it we can now get on with rehearsals.'

She called out to the others and Tom Marriott approached, a half wary, half quizzical expression on his face.

'Well, have you managed to sort her out?' he demanded.

Valma nodded and laughed. 'Just a little explaining was all that was needed. She'll be all right now, won't you?' she added with a glance at Kerry.

'Yes, I'll be all right,' Kerry replied, and involuntarily found her eyes going to Paul. He was looking down at her with the same quizzical expression that Tom Marriott wore, but without its wariness. She scowled at him blackly and his eyes glinted.

He crossed quickly to her side. 'You know, I have a suspicion you're still contemplating hitting me,' he whispered.

'All right,' Tom cut in. 'If you think you're sorted out now, we'll take it from where you come through the curtains.'

The two once more took their places in the tent as the others stood aback. Again Kerry watched Paul's face change until he was Marius once more and she felt the strange submerging feeling seep through her. Again Marius swept Layla up into his arms and shouldered his way through the curtains.

Kerry wasn't entirely submerged in Layla. She knew it was Paul carrying her and the fear with which she struggled against him was not all assumed. It made no difference to his hold of her and she was carried over and laid down amongst the cushions. As before he sat down by her side and leaned over her. She saw his dark face approach hers, saw again that wicked dancing smile. The moment his lips touched hers she was conscious again of the fiery tide that rushed through her, but this time she didn't try to fight it. She had the heady sensation of rushing out upon a dark glittering tide that was life itself, swimming in unknown and fathomless waters with no fear of sinking. Her lips quivered under his and answered their demand. Her arms went out to hold him.

Kerry could not have fought, even had she wanted to. All thought of an audience was forgotten. All feeling was centred in the warm strength of the man, in his caressing hands and forceful, demanding lips.

Very slightly he lifted his head. 'Is death still preferable, my little barbarian?'

As Layla, she drew his head down to her again and only dimly, as from another world, heard Tom Marriott's voice.

'O.K., cut,' he called out. 'Fifteen minutes' break.'

Kerry refused to look at Paul as he released her and stood up. She sat on the couch, her hands clenched in her lap, trying to still the wild throbbing of her senses and the quivering of her bruised lips.

For a while Tom was occupied giving orders for the next scene; the preceding short one faded back immediately to the main part of the film, although there were still the battle scenes to be done. When he turned back to them his eyes went from Kerry to the tall, black-haired actor with a strange expression.

'That scene won't want any more rehearsals. We'll shoot it tomorrow. After that we'll take the gypsy dance.'

'What do you intend doing this afternoon?' Paul asked, and Kerry wondered how he could make his voice so calm and even. She was still afraid to speak.

'We'll be doing crowd scenes and there's a sequence of the castle shots that will have to be re-done. I won't want you and Kerry. She's probably had enough for one day anyway. Same time tomorrow,' he added as he strode off to plunge into a discussion with one of the cameramen.

'I'll drive you home,' Paul said abruptly.

Meekly Kerry found herself following him to the car and climbing in beside him. He started the engine without speaking and swung the car away from the camp.

She sat as near to the door as she could get, yet it wasn't fear of him that sent her into that position, but a strange new shyness.

Kerry sat silently trying to analyse her

feelings. The thought of those few moments in the tent was still enough to quicken her breath and bring a flush to her face. If she allowed memory rein she could feel again the close hold of his arms and the quick fire of his lips on hers. It was unaccountable when for years she had despised such things. It was un-Kerryish. And unaccountable.

Or was it? Valma had said she was changing. Growing up, perhaps? Would other men's kisses arouse the same feelings? She didn't like the thought at all. It didn't have the pleasant excitement of her thoughts about Paul, but only gave her a vague feeling of disgust.

What if Kelvin kissed her like that? It didn't arouse disgust, but she couldn't imagine Kelvin kissing her as Paul had. It seemed silly that Kel, whom she had known all her life, should even contemplate such a thing. Only with Paul was the thought palatable.

She stopped there and wouldn't pursue the matter any further. Paul had also stopped the car.

He turned to look at her. 'Do you want to go straight home, or do anything else?' Again his voice had that odd abruptness.

Kerry hesitated. She was about to say she would like to go straight home, when she heard her own voice saying: 'I'd like to go swimming.'

It startled him out of his strange mood. 'You want to go swimming?'

'What's so strange about that?' she retorted defiantly. The idea, so unexpected even to her at first, had caught on and she was now quite prepared to defend it.

'Nothing strange at all,' he replied. 'Alone?'

Something in his voice startled her and she flashed him a quick look. He was staring straight in front of him and his profile was sharply etched and unreadable.

'Not necessarily.' Her voice was faintly troubled, wondering what was the cause of his strange attitude.

'I thought you would have had enough of me for one day.' His voice was still even and fairly expressionless, but she caught a faint undercurrent of something wistful and a little hurt. It bothered her, without knowing why. Like that other time she had sensed his need of her, she had, even unknowingly, to answer that need.

'What gave you that idea?' she asked carefully.

Quite suddenly Kerry moved nearer and one small, tanned hand slid under his as it lay on the wheel. She didn't know herself what caused the impulse. At any rate, her shyness had gone.

'I don't know what caused it, but please take that frightful scowl off your face, Paul,' she said coaxingly. 'I know a lovely place where we can swim.'

He started and the old devil-may-care smile broke over his face, the hand over hers tightened.

'Swimming it is, then. Where to, my lady?'

Kerry bit her lip undecidedly. 'Well, first I shall have to go home and pick up a swimsuit,' she said, 'and I suppose you'll have to go to Rylston for yours. It might be better to go to Rylston first and on to The House afterwards. It isn't much out of the way.'

'Valma probably has a swimsuit at the hotel you could borrow,' he suggested.

'I couldn't borrow one of hers,' Kerry objected. 'And anyway, she won't be at the hotel to ask.'

'We can telephone her at the camp,' he said, unperturbed. 'There's an emergency line out to it.'

She lapsed into an acquiescent silence as he turned the car towards Rylston, although she was secretly a little doubtful about wearing one of the sophisticated Valma's swimsuits. It would probably be rather scanty compared with the schoolgirlish black one she was used to. Especially with Paul, who seemed to have returned to normal again, if the pressure on her fingers was anything to go by.

It was strange, she thought, that when he was in a typical Devron mood she was wary of him, but immediately she sensed something wrong, should want to bring him back to it. One of the vagaries of growing up, perhaps? She dismissed it with a careless shrug, unknowing of what it portended. No girl could bear to see the man she loved hurt or unhappy, nor allow him to continue like it for long.

He drew up at the hotel and both went inside. It was no trouble getting Valma on the telephone and she gave Kerry instructions where to find a swimsuit, then spoke to the desk clerk and asked him to lend her spare key to the younger girl.

Kerry opened the door of the actress's room and, rather awed, looked around at the luxurious fittings and appointments of

Rylston's best hotel. When she opened the wardrobe where the swimsuit was supposed to be hanging, an involuntary gasp came from her at the sight of some of the clothes there. For a moment she couldn't resist taking out and looking at the beautiful things, then a little ashamedly she closed the door and opened the one on the opposite side. This section was filled half-way with polished drawers, but the top part was taken up by three swimsuits with matching beach coats, hanging from a small rail at the top.

Kerry eyed the swimsuits rather apprehensively. As she had feared, they were rather sophisticated. The worst of the lot was a white two-piece, beautifully made but, from appearances, quite revealing. A brilliant red one-piece would cover more, but she realized it would clash with her fiery hair and was unconsciously vain enough not to want that. The third, a plain green affair, was the nearest to the type of thing she was used to wearing. She lifted it down decisively. That would cover more of Kerry Derwin than the other two put together—well, almost.

She had almost reached the door when she suddenly turned and came back, replaced the green swimsuit and took down the white one. Before she could change her mind, surprised at her own daring, she went out quickly and locked the door behind her.

She found Paul waiting for her downstairs and handed the key back to the desk clerk before accompanying him outside. He took the white swimsuit from her with a lift of his eyebrows as he tossed it into the back of the car with his own swimming trunks and a couple of towels.

'Kerry, my sweet, you surprise me.'

Her mouth tilted impishly. 'I rather surprised myself,' she retorted lightly. He looked at her in a way that brought a warm flush to her face. 'And don't start getting ideas,' she added quickly.

Paul grinned. 'Not yet—I'll wait until I see you in that outfit!'

He opened the door for her and she climbed in and slid down in the seat until her head rested against the back of it. Paul took his place beside the wheel and twisted to look at her, bending over slightly, then he saw the alarm on her face and smiled.

'Don't worry. I wouldn't embarrass you by kissing you in Rylston's main street.' He started the car and added without looking round, 'Where to?'

She straightened up to direct him through the town, then pointed to a road leading across the moors.

'Just follow the road now. It isn't far and it goes straight to the coast.'

Paul drove fast and the powerful car ate up the miles under his expert control. Finally she roused herself to point out a rough turn off.

'We take this road now. The other one goes straight on to one of the big coastal towns. Very few people ever go to Deryl beach.'

This new road was almost as bad as the track that led to The House and on more than one occasion she was thrown violently against him. Paul, however, had his full attention on keeping the car on the road and Kerry smiled.

'This would be an occasion I could get even with you and you couldn't retaliate,' she commented to herself, but meaning him to hear.

'Don't you believe it,' he retorted. 'I wouldn't take long to stop the car, and in any case I take it we shall soon arrive at Deryl beach.'

Kerry, aware that he was quite capable of

stopping the car, subsided with a murmur about it not being fair.

The roadway finally petered out into a sandy track through sparse grass and ahead of them was the sea, brilliantly blue in the sunshine.

Kerry pointed to the left. 'If you can get along that way, there's an old hut we use for undressing.'

'We?' he questioned.

Kerry threw him a surprised look. 'Yes. Rick, Kel and I often used to come here.' She paused and added, 'We haven't been for a long time, now, though.'

'Why?' he asked, with his attention on negotiating the now non-existent road.

She shrugged. 'Rick went back to college for his final course and Kel has gone down to Cornwall.'

'You miss him, don't you?'

'Who—Kel?' When he nodded she looked surprised again. 'Why, of course. I've known Kel all my life.'

'Are you going to marry him eventually?'

She looked blank for a moment, then burst out laughing. 'Marry Kel? Of course not. I'm not going to marry anyone. Anyway, Kel wouldn't get such silly ideas. He's known me all my life.'

'Why don't you intend to get married?' he shot at her.

Kerry, taken by surprise, blurted out the truth. 'Because I don't like the idea of married life.'

The familiar quirk of one dark eyebrow was very much in evidence. 'Still being a coward and worrying about things beforehand?'

Kerry bristled. 'Certainly not! This is one thing my mind is really made up on.'

'How do you know?' he jeered. 'You made it up on other things and then found they weren't so bad after all.'

Her chin squared pugnaciously. 'You might have changed my mind about other things, but you're not bludgeoning me into getting married,' she retorted.

Paul grinned tauntingly as he stopped the car at the little hut. 'Wait until you're asked.'

She flushed hotly. 'I wasn't thinking of you,' she denied. 'I couldn't imagine being married to you, anyway.'

He twisted round to look at her and the glint was back in his eyes. 'Couldn't you, Kerry darling? Not if I laid my heart and fortune at your feet?' He reached out and took her hands. His voice was dangerously caressive, although laughter was still on his face and in his eyes. 'Marry me, Kerry. Let me teach you what love is.'

She gave him a suspicious look and tugged her hands free. 'Behave yourself! It would serve you right if I took you up on that, then sued you for breach of promise when you tried to wriggle out.'

'How do you know I would?' he questioned awkwardly. 'You might find yourself caught instead.'

She opened the door and slid out. 'From what I hear of you, my friend, you like variety.'

He climbed out too and stood looking at her, the bonnet of the car between them.

'I think being married to you would be variety enough.'

For one incredible moment she had a suspicion he was serious, but common sense quickly told her otherwise.

'Go and have a swim,' she replied, resorting to diversionary tactics. 'You'll realize what a lucky escape you had.'

Opening the back door of the car, she took out the white swimsuit and disappeared inside the little hut. Paul watched her go, smiling to himself.

Kerry, in the hut, was wishing now that

she had chosen the green swimsuit after all. The white one covered far too little of Miss Derwin. Not that there was anything remotely indecent about it. Like the white ballerina dress, it merely revealed more than she was used to showing. Luckily there was no mirror there or it was probable that she would have made some excuse not to go swimming after all.

Holding her neatly folded clothes in front of her as some measure of protection, she left the hut and approached the car. Under Paul's lazy, appreciative eyes she laid them in the back of the vehicle, taking a long while to do so and remarking, while still half in the car and obscured by it:

'The hut's all yours.'

Paul straightened up off the car and came round to the back to get his own trunks. As he opened the door his eyes smiled straight into hers, as she still carefully arranged her belongings.

'You can't hide in here forever, you know, you little coward,' he pointed out, then straightened up and strode to the hut.

She waited until he was safely inside, then ran for the sea. There she felt happier. The swimsuit was light and clinging and far more comfortable to wear than her own heavy woollen one, which had a tendency to stretch.

She turned over on her back and floated for a while. Her shyness vanished in dreamy content with the warmth of the sun on her face. The water felt soft and cushiony—like the divan in the tent this morning.

The sudden memory broke her calm and she turned over and began swimming quickly, as if she would out-distance her thoughts. That, however, was impossible. She knew that however long and far she swam, it would never be possible to lose the memory of those moments in the tent. Especially as she knew that, although it was the first time, it wasn't the last. This morning had only been the beginning of the film.

Yet did she really mind? It had been pleasant, as she had admitted to Valma, but Paul's other kisses had given her no hint of what to expect. She had been frightened, but also thrillingly alive as she had never been before. Strangely too, all strength had gone from her limbs, leaving them trembling and weak.

Paul's dark head appeared suddenly beside her. His hands reached out, gripped round her waist and pulled her under. She broke free from him and came up spluttering. For a moment she gave a bewildered shake of her head, but the moment his head broke water she reached out and determinedly thrust it under again. She couldn't escape retaliation, though. His arms caught her and again pulled her under with him.

They came up together, shaking the wet hair back out of their eyes, and Kerry turned and raced for the shore. As she neared the shallow water he caught up with her and swept her up into his arms, then a wave swept them both off their feet and threw them to the ground.

She sat up spluttering and laughing at the same time. Paul was just picking himself up too. He rested on one elbow, the other arm stretched across her, to prevent her escaping further. As his head bent towards her, another wave washed over them and she scrambled up and away from him.

'Serves you right,' she said, standing looking down at him, out of range of retaliation. 'Teach you to get amorous in the sea!'

Very unwarily, she turned her back and

began splashing up the beach. Behind her, Paul jumped to his feet and once again she was swept up into his arms, held high against him and completely helpless.

'Paul!' She beat on his bare, wet shoulder with ineffectual fists. 'Put me down!'

'Certainly,' he replied promptly, but instead of setting her on her feet, he laid her on the warm dry sand and stood looking at her.

Kerry recognized the tilt to his mouth and the laughter in his eyes that glinted darkly. She tensed, as if to run, although she knew it was impossible to escape on the deserted beach.

'Paul, don't you dare...!' she began warningly, and then realized her mistake. He promptly dropped down by her side and, as in the sea, one arm pinned her down, but this time there was no wave to come to her rescue.

'You should know by now that it isn't wise to dare me,' he said softly, and his lips were only a fraction away from hers.

She had no escape, or hope of escape. With a helpless little sigh, she raised her hands to his shoulders, slid them over the smooth, bare skin that was tanned to a coppery brown, and linked them together, holding him as he held her. The hard pressure of his lips was bruising hers, but she didn't care.

Kerry stirred, moving her hands on his back, liking the feel of the smooth, tanned skin beneath her fingers. Something at the back of her mind warned her that she would have a lot of explaining to do to herself later, but she was beyond caring at the moment. There was no room for anything else when his lips touched the hollow in her throat, then warm, seeking, moved back to her lips.

For some time they lay stretched out in the sun, drowsily content and talking only desultorily. Finally, her head pillowed on his shoulder and her hand resting on the arm that held her, she fell asleep. Last night, worrying about the part of Metani, there had been little rest for her.

It was late in the afternoon when Kerry moved her head restively, feeling somehow disturbed out of her peace.

'Have I been asleep?' she asked drowsily.

'Yes. Probably just sheer retaliation for me going to sleep on you once.'

Kerry sat up, shaking back her hair and staring moodily out over the sea, as if she was beginning to question the reason and cause of her feelings and it frightened her.

As if he knew what was in her mind, he pointed out across the sea to a small island, distracting her attention.

'What do they call that place?'

She started and followed the direction of his pointing hand. 'Torquil Island,' she answered. 'Nobody lives there but the gulls. It's a tiny place, but quite interesting. There are caves that Rick, Kel and I used to play in as children.'

'Children?' he jeered. 'What are you now?'

She sensed his change of mood and drew away from him, standing up with one graceful movement.

'Perhaps we could visit the island one day. I think we'd better be getting back home now, don't you?'

They dressed quickly and Paul drove her home in silence. When they reached The House he left Kerry with only a brief word of farewell. She wondered sadly if that golden afternoon would ever be repeated. Perhaps, in view of her own treacherous emotions, it might be as well if she avoided such outings in future, she resolved. But, in her heart of hearts, Kerry realized that it was not she but Paul, who would decide on their future relationship.

CHAPTER SEVEN

THE next time Kerry saw Barbie was the day Kelvin Treveryl returned to Rylston. As was her habit, it being a day when she wasn't wanted on the set, she rode into Rylston and left her horse at the Treveryl stables. Mallie had presented her with a formidable shopping list and Kerry had to hurry in order to get through it all before the shops closed. Barbie came into sight just as she was nearing the end of the list.

She stopped, allowing the younger girl to catch up with her. 'Hallo, Barbie.'

Barbie was panting slightly. She seemed even plumper and somehow younger.

'Hallo,' she answered, watching her friend interestedly. 'Where are you going?'

Kerry told her, making for the next stop in line. 'I've only a few more calls, then I shall have to be heading for home. Rick is coming back in a few days and Mallie's getting stocked up.'

Barbie looked even more interested. When she was not dreaming about Paul

Devron in a remote fairytale world, Kerry's twin was her ideal.

'It's a pity Kel isn't here now. We could have had one of our picnics,' Kerry commented slowly. She was beginning to realize how different things were. It was the first time it had actively crossed her mind. Before that the strenuous and exciting, if wearisome, work that filming had turned out to be had kept it from her notice, but now in a short respite of technical hitches at the set, it at last made itself fully known. Before Kel had always been there. Now he was away and Paul Devron was here.

Barbie looked at her strangely, as if the difference in her friend was becoming more pronounced, even to her.

'Kel's coming back today,' she said. 'Didn't you know?'

'Today?' Kerry threw her a surprised glance. 'No, I didn't know. Nobody mentioned it to me.'

'Well, you're not in Rylston much,' Barbie pointed out practically. 'They seem to keep you pretty busy out on the moors.'

There it was again. The gulf. 'We'll arrange a picnic,' Kerry said quickly. It was grasping at a past that was slipping from her, an attempt to regain the old, untroubled days when there had been no Paul Devron in her life to complicate it and make her feel restless and sometimes bewildered.

Barbie beamed happily. 'Gosh!' she exclaimed with fervour. 'I thought for a while that you wouldn't want to do anything like that again.'

Kerry frowned and moved uneasily. Her soft lips set and there was a hint of defiance in her eyes.

'What a ridiculous idea!' She consulted Mallie's list. 'I'll finish these off, then find out when Kel is due back.' She looked round at Barbie. 'Do you want to come with me, or shall I phone you at home when I've finished and been down to the stables?'

Barbie pouted consideringly. 'I'd better go home,' she decided.

Kerry walked quickly, finishing her shopping. For some reason she was beginning to be subject to a growing feeling of panic. Paul was occupying too many of her thoughts. It wasn't like Kerry Derwin to be so continually thinking of a man. And just lately, when she was away from him, she had been conscious of a sense of panic, as if she was caught in a tide that was bearing her to an unknown destination.

Paul had once asked her what she intended to do with her life if she didn't follow other girls' examples and marry. It was something Mallie also had asked her. But Mallie had also informed her that love would win in the end. Was that what was happening to her? Was it love laughing, as she herself had once laughed at love?

She shied away from it quickly. The idea was impossible. Then, if that was taboo, what did she want to do with her life? Oblivious of passers-by, she bit her lip mutinously and scowled. Her life was her own to do as she wanted with, in spite of other people having other ideas. The scowl grew. All right, so her life was her own. That still came back to the original question—what did she want to do with it? There must be some purpose in life for her. Did she always want to live at The House, helping Mallie, dancing sometimes in the quiet, sunlit room that had been her mother's? It was a life without purpose—even she realized that. There was her father and the affection between them, but even so, there had to be something else.

Set against all that, there was her part in the film. Perhaps there would be other roles after this one of Metani was finished, but that would mean leaving Rylston and entering a new world, one that she had already glimpsed in her work to date. In that world would be Paul Devron.

She muttered beneath her breath. Back to Paul Devron again! To the man who was probably the cause of her introspective argument with herself. Why must he colour her thoughts so much? Blindly, she refused to even think of the dangerous truth.

Even if the film company did offer her another part, perhaps it would be as well to refuse it. When they were gone life would return to normal again and if Paul really was the cause of her present unrest with life, normality would quickly return there too. Even though the acknowledgment of his effect on her was made, she still blindly refused to consider what lay underneath it. Anyway, she thought at last, it's a lovely day; too lovely to be bothered with such serious thinking. The future would take care of itself when it arrived. Worrying about things beforehand never improved matters. She would probably still be living at The House, living as she always had, no change, no worry, years later on and laughing at this odd period of unease in her life.

But that again returned to the old original question. What did she want to do with her life? Philosophically, she shrugged. Obviously at the moment she didn't know.

As she came in sight of the stables a taxi passed her and Kelvin Treveryl's dark head appeared at the window. A moment later it stopped and he got out.

She quickened her footsteps, her worries forgotten. 'Kel!'

Her eyes were shining and he smiled. 'I believe you seem pleased to see me.'

'Of course I'm pleased to see you.'

He gestured towards the open door of the taxi. 'Get in. You might as well finish the journey this way.'

She climbed in and he took his place beside her as the taxi started off again. She glanced at him then for some reason and quickly looked away again.

'Golden Ray has missed you,' she offered tentatively.

Kelvin smiled. 'Only Golden Ray?' His voice was teasing, but there was something else there as well that she couldn't understand.

'Well, of course we all have,' she added quickly.

'Thank you,' he said with a kind of dry grimness, and she looked up at him again. She wasn't the only one to have changed. As on the morning following the fancy dress ball, the signs were there, but now they were even more pronounced. Somehow his features had hardened. There was even a hint of grimness. His eyes were the eyes of a man. Kelvin Treveryl had something on his mind.

'I was coming over to try and find out when you would be back,' she rushed on, desperately trying to bring their relationship back to the old footing. 'Rick's coming back. I thought we might be able to arrange a picnic, like we used to.'

'Like we used to,' he echoed softly. 'Yes, it has changed, hasn't it, Kerry?'

She evaded looking at him. 'I don't know what you mean.'

'Yes, you do.' He smiled, still speaking quietly, so that their conversation was heard only by themselves. 'I told you once not to be on guard with me, Kerry. Don't run away from me either.'

Kerry swallowed hard and again avoided looking at him. This was a Kelvin Treveryl strange to her. She found she didn't know how to cope with him.

'Don't be silly. I'm not running away,' she denied with a shrug that was meant to be careless. 'How could one in a taxi? What was Cornwall like?'

He smiled again and allowed her to change the subject. 'Very rugged and lovely, but I'm glad to be back.'

'What did you do down there?' She was talking quickly, trying to keep the conversation impersonal.

'Learned a lot more about horses and running stables.'

He answered her questions good-naturedly, but all the time she had a feeling that he was waiting. When they reached the stables and he paid off the taxi he glanced down at her.

'Will you wait a few minutes while I change, Kerry? I'll ride a short way back with you.'

She forced an amused laugh. 'I won't get lost.'

'I'm not suggesting that you will. Nevertheless, I'll ride a way with you. There's something I want to talk to you about.'

'All right.'

She went round to the stables and waited there, stroking Smoky's smooth coat and trying not to think. 'Oh, Smoky,' she whispered into his silky mane, 'why does life have to get so complicated?'

Smoky turned his head and nuzzled her softly. She threw her arms around his neck with unconscious desperation.

'Why can't it be as it was? I don't want to change. I don't want my friends to change. Why don't things stay the same?'

'Because they can't, Kerry. The years bring changes to all of us. Sometimes it's quicker.' She had spun round at Kelvin's first words, but as she went to speak he shook his head and stopped her. 'Sometimes it's much quicker. Only months, perhaps even weeks or days. It can happen in even a brief second.'

'Kel . . .' Her hand went out protestingly, as if she would stop him saying what she instinctively guessed trembled on his lips, but he shook his head again.

'No, Kerry. You can't stop me saying it and I'm not ashamed of what's happened. I love you.'

Strangely then she felt in complete command of the situation. She couldn't speak for a long moment, though. She looked up at him, green eyes meeting blue and reading there what he felt for her. She knew the old Kerry Derwin would have been illogically indignant and angry and felt shame for that old Kerry Derwin. There was only pity now, pity and a growing sadness.

'I'm sorry, Kel,' she said quietly. 'It's no good, you know.'

He smiled very slightly. 'I know. But that didn't stop it happening.' His eyes searched her face, reading something there that crushed the last spark of hope in him. 'You've changed too, haven't you, Kerry?'

She fiddled with Smoky's mane and wouldn't meet his eyes. 'What do you mean?'

'I won't try to put it into words, because I know you understand what I mean.' He grasped her shoulders and turned her to face him, but she still refused to look up. 'Is it Devron, Kerry? Has he been making up to you?' As she moved uncomfortably in his hold and still refused to meet his eyes, his grip tightened. 'He has, hasn't he?'

She raised her eyes then, briefly, but dropped them again. 'Yes,' she admitted. 'I couldn't get out of it. They offered me a part in the film. We needed the money at home, so I . . . I accepted.'

Her voice trembled slightly on the last words, prosaic as they were, and the suspicion in his eyes, roused by jealousy, deepened.

'But not only on the film set?'

She twisted free, standing defensively against Smoky. 'Oh leave me alone, Kel!'

His eyes blazed and his hands went out to grip her shoulders roughly. 'No, I won't! What's he doing to you, Kerry?'

'He's not doing anything.' She tried again to twist free, but this time his hold was firm and unrelenting. 'We're merely making a film together. Just because I had to get over my aversion to being kissed, it doesn't mean that I'm falling in love with him.'

'Doesn't it?' he shot back. 'You little idiot, you're more than half in love with him already'. His voice softened and his eyes were pleading as he held her a little way from him to look down into her face. 'Don't fall in love with him, Kerry. He's not good for you. What you feel is only infatuation. He has that effect on thousands of women.'

Her eyes flashed. 'Once again, I'm not falling in love with him,' she retorted furiously.

'Please try to understand.' The urgency in his voice deepened. 'I admit I'm jealous, but I don't want you to be hurt. That's the main reason why I'm acting like this.'

Her eyes fell to the floor again. Some of her indignation abated. With the toe of one polished boot she scuffed the floor, but although anger had gone, the chaos and confusion came back.

She had come to the Treveryl stables to recapture the uncomplicated friendship of her old life and instead found more change. A Kelvin Treveryl who had returned to her a complete stranger. A Kerry Derwin who was equally changed. He was right. Change could not be halted. It had to come and give place to yet other changes with the years. It only brought bewilderment to try to live in a past that didn't exist any more.

Yet the present was too disturbing. It was like being in a misty room, trying to pierce the gloom to find what she had to become accustomed to, or standing on a path out on the moors, with the white mists around her, looking round, trying to recognise the countryside, to place the dangers of quagmire and the safety of firm trails. To her life suddenly seemed like that. It was a trail. Part of it was behind her, clearly defined, known and familiar. But that was the past and she had to go on, treading an unfamiliar and dangerous path that led to somewhere. A haven at each end. The House she had left. Somewhere at the end of the shrouded path was . . . what?

Kelvin shook her slightly. 'Come back, Kerry.' He released her and smiled. 'I promise to behave myself.'

She flashed him a quick upward look, then away again, biting her lips.

'What is it?' he questioned softly.

Something was going through her mind. It was a fear that had to be quietened and there was only one way to do it.

'Will you kiss me, Kel?'

He started at her strange request, at least it seemed strange coming from her, then pulled her gently into his arms. While she waited for him to kiss her, her mind raced. He had said she was falling in love with Paul. This would prove him wrong. More, it would prove to herself that he was wrong.

His kiss was gentle and shy and it left her completely unmoved. A feeling of panic went through her and she linked her arms around his neck, pressing herself closer against him and trying to force herself to feel what she had when Paul kissed her.

Kelvin kissed her again, more passionately this time, as if he sensed her complete indifference to him emotionally, but it was no use.

The panic in Kerry's mind became stark fear. There was none of the fire and excitement of Paul's kisses. The feel of Kelvin's lips was quite pleasant, but that was all. Only Paul had the power to rouse her to the mad, tumultuous emotion that left her limp in his arms. Only Paul's lips, sensuous and questing, could demand a response from hers.

She broke free from Kelvin and leaned her head against Smoky with a broken sob.

Kelvin put out a hand, as if to touch her, but drew it back. 'Kerry . . .' He stopped and winced. 'Kerry, please don't. I didn't mean to frighten you.'

She swung round. Her face was as white as Paul's had been. 'Frighten me?' For a moment she didn't understand, then she laughed bitterly, careless and forgetful of hurting him. 'You didn't frighten me, Kel. You didn't kiss me like he did—but he didn't frighten me either. I . . . I liked it.'

Kelvin stiffened, then he drew her gently against him. 'It's no use denying it, darling.' His voice was very soft and sad as he stroked her bright hair. All thought of his own loss was for the moment gone in the unhappiness he read in her eyes. 'He does have some effect on you, whether it's love or only infatuation. I hope for your sake that it's infatuation. You can get over that.'

'No!' It was a desperate cry of denial. 'No, he doesn't!' She turned on him and battered at his chest with frantic fists. 'No, Kel! He doesn't. I want to stay free. I don't want to fall in love.'

'You can't help it,' he answered sadly. 'It's something that just happens. I can't tell you whether it's infatuation or love. If it's infatuation, it will go.'

Kerry gulped and sniffed unconsciously as she raised tear-drenched eyes to his.

'What can I do?' she asked brokenly.

'Do?' He shook his head. 'There's nothing you can do. As for Devron . . .' He broke off and a shadow clouded his eyes. 'I've only met him once, on the night of the fancy dress ball, but I'm not too blinded by jealousy to admit that I found him likeable, even then. I don't think he would have made love to you just idly, and being in love with you myself, I somewhat naturally believe that other men would want to marry you as well. No, Kerry. Although above all things I want your happiness, I'm afraid I can't tell you what to do.'

She drew away from him and determinedly scrubbed at her eyes with a handkerchief.

'Oh well,' she said with an air of forced practicability, 'I shall just have to wait and sort things out.' Her voice softened and she laid a hand on his arm. 'I'm sorry, Kel, about you.'

He smiled and shook his head. 'It's not your fault. I'll just go on hoping that it's infatuation you feel for Devron, so I might have a chance afterwards. Now,' he continued with a brisk change of subject that hid what he was feeling, 'I'd better get you home or Mallie will be sending out search parties!'

Following his mood, Kerry determinedly thrust away the unhappy and disturbing thoughts that were bothering her mind and helped him strap the bags containing Mallie's shopping on to Smoky's saddle, then waited while he saddled Golden Ray. Leading the two horses, they went outside and mounted.

For a time they rode in silence. Even though only a short time before she had thrust them from her, Kerry found her uneasy thoughts returning.

Was Kelvin right? Was she in love with Paul?

She had no experience to tell whether it was love or infatuation, if it was either she felt, but she only had to think of him and a tremor would run through her. She thought of denying everything to herself and burying her head ostrichlike, as she had in the beginning, but with true Derwin honesty she at last had to admit the reality of her feelings. It might not be pleasant or palatable to realize that she was either in love or infatuated, but the fact remained that she was. Nor did she like to think that it was merely infatuation. It didn't feel like infatuation—but then she didn't know what love felt like. All she knew was that she suddenly wanted Paul at her side. A coldness shivered up her spine as she allowed her thoughts to go on from there. What about Paul? He had admitted that he enjoyed making love to her, but that was not love. He was rich and famous. With that very potent fascination he had for women, there were many equally rich and famous ones, beautiful women, that he could choose a wife from. Kerry Derwin was very unglamorous and usual compared with them. It was beyond imagination that he should fall in love with and want to marry someone as ordinary as herself.

Some of the old belligerent anti-romance of the old Kerry Derwin came to life and very sternly told her that she didn't ever intend to get married. She observed and contemplated it for a moment, then sadly but honestly told herself that it was out of date. She did want to get married, and she wanted to marry Paul Devron, of all people.

* * *

During the next couple of days work on the film set Kerry saw very little of Paul. They were filming the scenes where she was supposed to be brooding over ancient spells on the island in the bog, where Lady Frances came to beg her to give up the gypsy.

There was an eerie fascination about it that played on her nerves, so much so that at one time she wondered whether such spells would bind a man. At the times she did see Paul he was strangely moody and irritable. She had the strange idea that he was avoiding her. Stranger still, it hurt. Perhaps she really was in love with him.

She was preparing to go home one day, when her part in the filming was completed early, when Paul came up and grasped her arm.

'Come along, young lady. You promised to show me Torquil Island some time. This is the time.'

'But . . .' she began, surprised.

'No buts,' he said firmly. 'You're not doing anything else, are you?'

'No, only . . .' She broke off and blinked. 'All right.'

Meekly she allowed herself to be installed in his car and told him which direction to take to reach the island. It was rather a silent drive and she sensed that he had something on his mind. When they reached the small cove adjoining Deryl beach, where they had gone last time, it was easy enough to hire a small rowboat, as Kerry had done many times before when she had gone to the island with Rick and Kelvin.

The sea was slightly choppy, but Paul managed the small boat with ease. She knew the hidden strength in that long, lean body. The silence was still between them and it was a strange silence, compounded of contentment in each other's presence and something strained underneath.

When they reached the island she pointed out the little rocky landing stage fashioned by nature and he brought the rowboat alongside it. After tying the boat to a piece of rock, he stepped out and helped her over the slippery rocks. Then he stooped down and picked up the packet of food that lay at the bottom of the boat.

'There's a good view from the top of the hill,' Kerry suggested. She spoke rather quickly and for some reason her voice was breathless. Some inner tension was beginning to build up. Every now and again she met Paul's eyes and something in their expression made her uneasy. At times they had the old devil glint, then they would become brooding, or again a hint of dark storm would enter their blackness, as if momentarily a rein slipped and something of what was underneath boiled up.

'Very well. We'll go to the top,' he agreed, and almost immediately, to her astonishment, he became the old Paul Devron, laughing and teasing her.

They reached the top of the hill and

looked around them. From there the island seemed very tiny and the seas much rougher than they had been only a few minutes ago. Kerry frowned as she looked downwards. She knew how suddenly the storms could arise in this district.

'What's the matter?' Paul asked, seeing her frown.

'I think there's going to be a storm,' she answered. 'Perhaps we shouldn't have come out this afternoon.'

He looked up at the sky, but it was still clear. Kerry shook her head and pointed to the sea.

'It's choppy. The sky will cloud over soon. It can get rough here sometimes. I think we should leave soon. We can explore it another day.'

Even as she spoke, a dull rumble sounded in the distance and he nodded.

'We'll get back to the boat straight away.'

The sky began to cloud over and as they descended the hill the first few drops of rain fell. Kerry stopped and shook her head. The sea was rougher than ever now.

'I don't think we'd better chance it. The boat would never stand up to the sea as it becomes when there's a storm. There are caves here we can shelter in. The storms usually blow over very quickly, although they're exceedingly violent while they last.'

They barely had time to reach the caves she led the way to before the rain came down in blinding sheets. Both ducked inside and Paul looked round interestedly.

'I believe they used to be smugglers' caves,' she informed him. 'There are three connecting ones. Kel and I . . .'

Paul suddenly stiffened and swung round. 'Yes, Kel?' he questioned softly, dangerously. 'You're fond of him, aren't you, Kerry?'

Taken by surprise, Kerry looked up at him with confirmation in her face. 'Yes,' she admitted.

'Why?'

He shot the word at her and again her surprise was evident on her face. She wondered where all this was leading to.

'We're old friends . . . Paul!' The last was an exclamation of pain. He had grasped her arms with hurtful force. When she looked up his face was pale, but his eyes were blazing. They were dangerous. She swallowed hard and bit her lips. 'Paul—what's the matter?'

'What's the matter!' he bit out tersely,

and the thin thread of savagery in his tone sent a little shiver of frightened excitement through her.

He pulled her into his arms and kissed her, bruising her lips and hurting her body with the fierce strength of his hold.

'Do you love him, Kerry?' His voice was thick and husky with passion and without giving her a chance to answer he kissed her again. 'You wouldn't dare, Kerry. You belong to me. You'll marry me, not Kelvin Treveryl or anybody else.'

Almost fainting, Kerry turned her head away from him and drew great breaths of air into her aching lungs. Her lips stung for the hard pressure of his and her senses were whirling until she couldn't think at all.

'No,' she whispered at last.

His grip tightened cruelly and the fire in his eyes blazed out at her.

'No?' he echoed curtly. 'It's yes, Kerry. Whether it's against your will or not, you're going to marry me. This thing between us is too great to be crushed out because you're a coward.'

'But, Kelvin . . .' she began, meaning to try to explain somehow, if she could sort out her words, that she had no intention of marrying Kelvin, but he cut across her words.

'Damn Kelvin!' he swore furiously. 'You're going to marry me,' and he began kissing her again, but this time it was different from any other time. This time he had to prove to her why she must marry him, why they needed each other. His hands were moving on her shoulders and back with a peculiar caressing movement that brought a choking sensation to her throat and his lips on hers were more sensuously demanding than they had ever been before. The shivering excitement his kisses always roused became a sharp pain that tore at her and made her press closer to him with a little helpless moan.

More gently now, he pressed her head against him, holding her quietly. Her hands still clung to him and her soft voice came broken and husky.

'Paul . . . Paul . . .'

He didn't answer, just held her to him and softly stroked her hair back off her face, as Kelvin once had, but she hadn't shivered in Kelvin's arms as she did in his, shivered with unsatisfied desire.

For long moments they stood there in silence, then Paul at last spoke. 'You're going to marry me, Kerry.'

'Yes.' Her voice was the merest whisper of sound that dropped yet lower in shyness. 'You haven't said you love me.'

She heard him laugh softly. 'You little idiot! I fell in love with you at the fancy dress ball. You'll never know how near you were to being kissed that night.'

She looked up at him then, her eyes round with surprise. 'As long ago as that?'

He nodded. 'As long as that. I didn't have a chance from the moment you swiped that hat away from me.'

The old familiar grin crinkled her face. 'The head of the household lectured Rick and me good and proper for that stunt, but it was worth it.' The grin died and she twisted a button on his coat, watching it with concentrated attention. 'I shall take an awful teasing now, I suppose.'

'Can't you take it?' He made her look up at him and a shade of grimness crossed his face. 'You'd better, because you won't get out of marrying me, young lady.'

The button came off in Kerry's hand and she gave it a surprised look. Paul took it from her and dropped it into a pocket.

'Just for pulling that off, you can sew it on again. I'll save it until we're married.'

She laughed and rubbed her head against

him like a contented kitten. 'I think I'm beginning to rather like the idea,' she admitted. 'Being married, I mean.'

His arms tightened around her. 'I'll do everything I can to make you like it, Kerry darling.'

Some time later they both became aware that the rain had abated. It still drizzled greyly, but they went to the mouth of the cave to survey their surroundings. Paul frowned as he looked from the clouded sky to the still turbulent sea.

'I wonder if we ought to chance getting back now,' he said thoughtfully.

Kerry peered around. 'We could, I suppose.' She sounded a little doubtful. 'It could be on the point of clearing up or starting worse than ever. When it does that, it usually sets in for the night or a couple of days.'

'I'd better go down and see if the boat is all right in any case.'

She watched him picking his way down the slope that led to the little inlet where they had left the rowboat. Then she looked up at the sky again and down at the sea. She wasn't worrying too much about being kept at the island by the storm for an extra hour or two. The only trouble was that Mallie and her father would be anxious if she was late. There was nothing that could be done, however. The storms in this locality were pretty peculiar in their characteristics, but they showed a certain constancy that enabled the local inhabitants to plan their movements during the stormy season. This particular specimen would continue for another couple of hours, alternately just drizzling and storming, but the waves would gradually grow smaller. If on the other hand it was to be one of the rarer, really violent storms, there would be a break of about half an hour, perhaps a little longer, when sky and sea would look deceivingly innocent, then the storm would return, violently.

Paul was away rather a long time. It stopped raining and the sun came out again. Kerry cast a suspicious look at the smiling sky and went to find him. This had every aspect of a violent return. They would just have time to reach the mainland before it broke.

She reached the tiny bay and looked round quickly, trying to see where he had gone. 'Paul, the boat . . .'

He came into sight around the rocks, wiping his hands on a handkerchief. His face was grim.

She ran up to him quickly. 'What's happened?'

'The boat is smashed on the rocks,' he answered tersely. 'It must have drifted away during the storm.' His mouth set hard in self-contempt. 'I should have fastened it more securely.'

She shook her head. 'You don't know the currents here. I should have warned you that they'll tear a boat loose, especially in a storm.' She looked down to where the row-boat had been and then up to him again. 'What are we going to do?'

His eyes narrowed, measuring the distance to the mainland. 'I suppose I could swim it.'

Instantly something cold went through her. If she hadn't realized it before, she would have known at that moment that she loved him. There was very little chance of even a strong swimmer reaching the mainland. The currents around the island were treacherous and there was the chance, almost a certainty now by the look of the sea, that the storm would return. A boat could make it in time, but not a swimmer. Anyone caught in those tossing, deadly seas would never reach the mainland. But Paul wouldn't be stopped by that, instinctively she guessed it. Only guile would keep him on the island.

'Swim it?' she echoed quickly. 'No, Paul! Please don't leave me here alone. I'm terrified of storms.' He turned to look at her in surprise and she swallowed hard and clutched at his arm, thanking heaven for Marriott's training. It had to be good, though, to deceive Paul, experienced actor as he was, but at least he had no reason to suspect her of putting on an act.

His fingers closed over hers as it lay on his arm. 'There's nothing to worry about, Kerry. You'll be all right if you stay in the cave.' He gave her hand a reassuring squeeze and laughed, 'After all, it's not one of our film islands that sprout volcanoes and blow up!'

Kerry deliberately made her answering smile self-conscious and ashamed. 'I know I'm an idiot,' she admitted, 'but I get the jitters. Please stay, Paul.'

As if to help her, ahead of time, thunder rolled warningly in the distance and provided her with the opportunity to throw herself into his arms and hide her head against him.

'All right.' He gave in with a smile, not

proof against her clinging hands. 'I'll stay here, then, but I hope the old man we borrowed the boat from will send someone out to us.'

Having won her point, Kerry was prepared to agree with him. 'Oh, he will,' she agreed instantly. 'Only I just couldn't stand being left here alone in the storm, and it's on the way back all right.'

They started to walk back towards the cave, going slowly as it had not yet started to rain again, although the sky was already clouding over again and the waves were pounding the rocks. Every now and again, though, Paul threw her a puzzled glance, which at last became openly suspicious.

'You know, I have a funny idea you're playing a part, my sweet,' he said with a sideways look at her. Thunder rolled across the heavens again, menacingly nearer, and he grasped her shoulders and turned her to look at him. 'I don't believe you're really in the least afraid of the storm.'

Lightning flashed and the thunder came still nearer. The sky was darkening and the wind began to whistle around the island. It was too late for him to change his mind now and decide to try to reach the mainland after all.

She smiled up at him mischievously. 'Not in the least afraid,' she admitted blithely. 'As a matter of fact, I rather like storms.'

'You little devil!' he exclaimed softly. 'What was the idea . . .?'

'I didn't want you to go.' Her smile died and she bit her lips. 'I know these seas. You wouldn't have got an eighth of the way by now and in a few minutes the storm will really start.'

Paul looked at her intently. The colour rose to her face and her eyes fell before his. Then he smiled, with the dancing glint in his eyes.

'Well, I must admit to feeling rather flattered by your reason. You've never admitted that you cared for me, even though you've agreed to marry me.' His voice softened and his hands on her shoulders drew her closer to him. 'You do, don't you, Kerry? I haven't merely bludgeoned you into agreeing to marry me?'

Shyness overwhelmed her and she hid her face against his shoulder, muttering something indistinctly.

'Kerry, this is one thing you must answer. I know I rushed things this afternoon, I was jealous of Kelvin, but you do love me, don't you?'

Kerry's reply was whispered so low he hardly heard it, but it satisfied him.

They stayed in the vicinity of the caves until the rain started again, which it didn't take long in doing. After that the heavens quite simply opened. With their arms about each other they watched from the entrance of the cave. The thunder grew intense and rolled directly overhead. Lightning lit up the cave and then passed on, leaving the storm still raging. Angry wind whistled about the island, whipping the waves into a maddening dance, and incessantly the rain teemed down.

It grew late, but at last the storm showed signs of abating. They waited some time in the cave and fought for a while about Kerry taking Paul's coat, but in the end he won. Then faintly, across the sea, came the noise of a voice calling to them, and the sound of their rescue party approaching.

CHAPTER EIGHT

THE thing that surprised Kerry most was the fact that, while Rylston exhibited the expected amazement, both her father and Mallie took it in their stride when told that she was to marry Paul. They were obviously pleased though and neither one of them made any teasing remarks.

Kerry was perhaps the most astounded herself. Without knowing how it happened, she found herself engaged to be married. There were moments when she pinched herself, just to make sure that she was not having some sort of peculiar dream. After all, she was Kerry Derwin, who had once sworn never to get married. The same Kerry Derwin who had once been so scornful about 'the idol of the silver screen, the great lover himself, the original pitter-patter of a million dreaming hearts . . .' Sometimes she smiled ruefully to herself as she recalled her scathing words to Barbie, words that had been spoken not so very long ago as time was measured. It was fantastic that she could have changed so much, but there was no doubt about it.

Love was getting the laugh that had been gathering for quite a while.

The filming of *Moorland Duel* was proceeding well, with a new ease and absence of irritability that was only slightly upset by the publicity attendant upon so well known a star as Paul Devron becoming engaged.

They had decided to get married when the film was ended, but Kerry found her feelings becoming very complicated and mixed when she thought of the nearing completion of her role of Metani. Although she knew she loved Paul, she still hadn't overcome entirely her old fears of marriage. Somewhere in the back of her mind they lurked, waiting. At unguarded moments they stabbed her with a feeling of panic. The first time was when Paul had slid the beautiful emerald ring on to her finger and she had felt the possession in his touch and seen it in his eyes. It had gone away, but now and again it came back. Those were the times she thought, half reluctantly, of breaking the engagement, but such chaotic and rather bewildered plans didn't get very far. She had a suspicion too that Paul wouldn't have let her break it.

Kelvin she saw only once more. He came

to The House while she was out in the tangled gardens, picking flowers from the riot of colour that ran wild there. She didn't know he was watching her until she turned suddenly to cut a rose and found him standing there.

'Kel!' She carefully detached herself from the thorny rose her sudden movement had caused her to become entangled with. 'I didn't hear you arrive.'

'I only just came on the scene,' he said quietly, and smiled. 'Don't worry, I haven't been standing watching you for long.'

Kerry looked down at the square emerald that flashed in its delicate setting.

'You know I'm going to marry Paul?'

'I know.' He smiled again and held out his hand to her. 'Congratulations, Kerry. Even though I've seen very little of him, I know you'll be happy with him.'

Kerry grasped his hand with both of hers. 'I know I shall be.' Her grip tightened on his hand. 'But what about you, Kel?' A cloud shadowed the happiness in her eyes and he laughed whimsically.

'No waterworks, redhead. I'll insult you and say I'll get over it.'

Even against her will her lips trembled.

It seemed all wrong that Kelvin, whom she had known for so long, should have to be hurt like this.

'I wish it didn't have to be like this,' she said aloud.

'It's not your fault, Kerry. These things just happen. I'm not denying that it hurts, it does badly, but I'll get over it, or at least I shall try to. It's a case of necessity. You and Paul are a pair—I can see that now. Even if I had the power to, I wouldn't want to try to alter it.'

'What are you going to do?'

'I'll go back to Cornwall, I left early in any case.'

'You're going back straight away?'

'Straight away,' he confirmed. 'Don't ask me to your wedding, Kerry. That's something I would be too much of a coward to do.' He saw the mistiness in her eyes and forced a smile that was remarkable in its gaiety and took one of the roses from her. 'I told you no tears, redhead.' He flicked her cheek lightly with the velvet petals of the rose. 'Good luck!' Then he was gone.

Kerry stood quite still, while the tears ran unheeded down her cheeks. She saw him turn between two large elms, the sun glinting on his hair, then he passed behind a large overgrown hedge and was out of sight. But still she stood there, the flowers clutched tightly in one hand, careless of thorns sticking into her fingers from the roses.

A hand came from behind her and rescued the ill-treated flowers. 'You'll really mangle those poor flowers, child,' her father's voice commented.

Kerry gulped and turned round. For a moment she looked at him, then threw herself into his arms and began to sob violently on his shoulder. He held her gently, looking over her brilliant head towards where Kelvin Treveryl had disappeared, and his eyes were sympathetic.

Kerry cried like a child for a while, but as the storm showed signs of dying down, he shook her chidingly.

'That's enough, young Kerry. Mop them up now. Kelvin has taken it far better than you have.'

She raised a tear-drenched face to him. 'Why did I have to hurt him like this?'

'It was something neither of you could help. And he was right about getting over it, you know.' A curiously enigmatical look came over his face. 'What I'm going to say now may sound a little too poetical and fantastic in our rather prosaic modern age, but I believe it and if you can too, it will help you over Kelvin and also with regard to your feelings for Paul, which I suspect are still a little mixed up.' He paused and then went on seriously, 'I believe in affinity, Kerry. Every man and woman has a true affinity for only one other person. If they're lucky, if they find that person, they are the ones who know the great heights and the great depths of the world. Their life is never the same again. I was one of those lucky people.'

As he paused Kerry drew a quivering breath. 'You mean, many people really only take second best?'

'They never know it's second best. But that doesn't mean that they're not happy. They could be extremely happy all their lives, physically and mentally attracted to each other, and never know it was second best until they met that other kind of love, if ever. I think that you and Paul are among the lucky ones.'

'But how does anyone know it is this . . . affinity love?' Her eyes were very young and bewildered as she looked up at him.

He shook his head. 'There's no way of

telling, Kerry, not at first, just as in the beginning it's hard to tell love from infatuation. When you've faced adversity in your marriage for the first time you'll know which it is.' He saw the look that crossed her face and smiled. And as Kerry walked with her father through the overgrown garden back to The House, for the first time in weeks a brooding sense of hurt was gone from her.

* * *

The film was finished. The main scenes had already been shot before they had started on the scenes Kerry was in.

It had been hard and strenuous work at times, but she had enjoyed it. There was a stirring moment when, as Layla, she drove a battle chariot against the enemy Romans. They had to teach her how to handle the chariot, but she needed no lessons for the moments when, in her witch girl costume, she rode over the moors, her hair streaming behind her in mad abandon. But the one part she liked above all others was the wild gypsy dance she did with Paul.

The film was finished. She repeated it to herself. That meant in three weeks she would be married. There was a frightened excitement in the thought.

But next in line was the party. Paul told her about it with the impudent grin she knew so well.

'We're going to have a party.'

They were eating sandwiches at the mobile canteen of the company, at what would probably be their last visit there, and Kerry gave him a questioning look.

'What sort of a party, and who's having it?'

'We are. We always have one at the end of a film. Everybody wears one of the costumes they wore in the film.'

Her eyes sparkled. 'Lovely,' she said delightedly. 'Where's it being held?'

He leaned across the little table, watching her with a look that made her colour rise.

'At a certain place that has a disused second balcony where a frightened redhead once took refuge.'

'At the Hall!' Then the meaning of the latter part of the sentence sank in. The old belligerent look squared her chin. 'I wasn't frightened!' she retorted indignantly.

'No?' he jeered. 'Then why did you run and hide upstairs? You took flight the moment you saw I'd come back.'

'I was merely taking no chances,' she said, and gave him a sideways look that dared him to comment further.

'I don't blame her running,' Valma put in from behind them. 'If I remember rightly, you had a very dishonourable look in your eyes at the time, Paul.'

Kerry twisted round in her chair. 'I wasn't running,' she repeated with pugnacious insistence.

'Then it was a good imitation,' Paul retorted.

'And if you weren't, you should have been,' Valma added.

Kerry gave both of them an exceedingly wary look.

'By the way,' Valma continued, serious now, 'I'm going shopping this afternoon. Would you like to come with me? You probably have one or two things to get yourself.'

Kerry nodded eagerly. 'Yes, I would. I don't know very much about buying girls' things.'

Paul's intensely dark eyes went over his fiancée slowly, with such an appreciative and intent regard that she felt herself beginning to tremble. Those two expressive black eyes that said far more than could ever be put into words.

'Paul, stop it!' she said breathlessly.

'Stop what?' His voice was lazily amused.

'You know what you're doing,' she retorted. 'So why should I tell you?'

'And why should I stop?' He didn't. He went on looking at her in the same way.

Valma decided it was time she rescued her.

'Finished your lunch?' She stood up. 'Good. Then we'll go and do our shopping and leave him here.'

'All on my own?' He sounded too plaintive to be true and Kerry's grin spread over her face.

'Serves you right!' she told him, and went off with Valma.

Valma's car was smaller than Paul's, and, surprisingly for such a sophisticated woman, was an open sports model. Quite unashamedly its dark blue colouring was exactly that of her eyes. Its upholstery was a light silvery grey and beautifully kept.

As they climbed in, Valma threw the younger girl an approving glance. Kerry was wearing one of the dresses she had bought with her first cheque. Dark green and trimly tailored, it gave her an unusual air of sophistication. Only her hair was unchanged; rioting free in its old gay abandon, it gave a pixy impudence to the sophistication.

'That's a new dress, isn't it?' Valma inquired as she started the car, and when Kerry nodded, she added: 'You have good taste. You won't need to learn what to buy.'

Kerry smiled shyly and changed the subject. Compliments always embarrassed her. She was still too young to have learned to accept them gracefully.

'Where are we going?' she asked. 'Rylston?'

'No, I think we'll go to Exeter,' the actress replied. 'Much as I like your little town, there's not much opportunity for shopping.'

They drove for some time in semi-silence, chatting desultorily when something took their notice. Valma drove fairly fast but competently, intent on the road, yet at same time dreamily content.

Kerry watched her unobtrusively, wondering what was putting the dreamy content in the lovely blue eyes. Was it a man? She didn't realize she had said it aloud, until Valma shot her a startled look.

'Yes, it's a man.' A mischievous smile twitched her lips. 'He's tall, Kerry, and dark-haired. His eyes are dark too and I think he's the most wonderful man in the whole world.'

The description fitted Paul. A feeling she had never experienced before crawled up Kerry's spine. It was uncomfortable and decidedly unpleasant. Her hands clenched in her lap and she couldn't help her whole body stiffening.

Valma gave a delightful burst of laughter. 'His eyes are dark grey, not black, you jealous little idiot! I mean my husband.'

Kerry flushed, feeling childish, and looked shamefacedly down at her hands as they slowly relaxed.

'I wasn't thinking . . . I mean I . . .'

'Oh yes, you were,' Velma retorted in complacent amusement. 'I meant you to.'

'You meant me to?' Kerry echoed her words in amazement. 'But why?'

'To remind you that you're in love with Paul.'

She had a wary 'on guard' look and avoided meeting Valma's eyes. Half absently, looking out over the moors, she noted that the outskirts of civilization were in view.

'I don't understand what you mean,' she said carefully.

'Don't you?' Valma still had her eyes on the road and the smile had died from her face. 'Once or twice I gained the impression that you've been trying to persuade yourself that you've been coerced into this marriage against your will.'

The elder woman's uncanny perception again startled her. There had been such occasions, when the old fears of marriage returned and she had frantically tried to find some loophole of escape.

'It hurt, didn't it, to think that somebody else might be in love with Paul the way you feel, even though you may at times try to convince yourself that you don't love him. You know that if anybody else loved him as you do, they would want him for their own. And that's frightening, isn't it? You wouldn't want to lose him, would you, Kerry?'

Kerry saw that her hands had again gripped themselves together in her lap. It seemed they had a volition of their own. Almost against her will she contemplated what Valma had said.

'No, I wouldn't want to lose him,' she

said at last, very quietly.

'And that leads me to another thing,' Valma drew into the side of the road and stopped the car. There she turned in the seat and looked directly at the girl. 'When you get to Hollywood, possibly before then, you'll hear all sorts of rumours.'

'Linking your name with Paul?' she asked, trying to fight down what she now knew to be jealousy.

'Yes.' Valma admitted it unhesitatingly. 'Whatever you hear, there'll be nothing in it. Paul and I are good friends, but that's all. I told you once before that I'm very much in love with my husband.' She threw Kerry a whimsical look. 'If I had Bruce with me, I doubt whether I would see your Paul, even if he was in the same room.' Her expression became serious again. 'But you'll possibly find his name linked with his leading lady in every film he makes. It's just a way that gossip has. Don't forget also that if you continue with your own career, it will start on you too.'

Kerry's eyes opened wide. 'You mean people will say that I'm having affairs with other men? How ridiculous!' she added indignantly.

Valma smiled. 'Being Kerry Derwin,'

she said, 'you've probably made up your mind that only Paul shall kiss you, and I pity poor Tom if he ever tries to make you change your mind, but the gossips don't care about anything like that. So, you see, it will be on both sides.'

As she started the car again, Kerry slid further down in the seat. Her expression was very pensive. She had a lot to think about.

By the time they arrived at the outskirts of Exeter hardly half a dozen words had been spoken between them since Valma re-started the car, yet it had been a friendly silence.

Valma pulled up in a side street and reached for a scarf which she tied carelessly over her hair, and then produced a pair of dark glasses.

Kerry chuckled. 'Is this your disguise?'

Valma nodded ruefully. 'It may sound conceited, but sometimes it's necessary.' She put the glasses on and opened the door. 'We'll leave the car here, out of the way. I have an idea the publicity hounds have been photographing it.'

They left the rakish little blue car looking out of place in the quiet, sedate district and caught a bus for the centre of the town. It was evident from Valma's purposeful lead as they alighted from the bus that she had been shopping in Exeter before. She knew just where to go.

As they paused at the portals of a large and exclusive dress shop, Kerry felt a little thrill of awe. It was rather unbelievable to find that she was in a position to go shopping at one of such stores, and in the company of a world-famous actress. However, the money burning a hole in her handbag assured her that it was no dream. She felt the beginning of an exciting thrill of anticipation. There was a very feminine glint in her eyes as she looked round.

A slim, gaunt creature in unrelieved and extremely sophisticated black swam towards them over the thick pile of the silver grey carpet.

'Ah, Mademoiselle Valma. This is a pleasure.'

'First we would like to see some evening gowns,' Valma replied, and seated herself in one of the grey leather chairs.

'Ah, but certainly.'

Madame Antoinette prided herself in being the only shop in the district at that time possessing two mannequins. She advertised the fact widely, charged exorbitant prices on quite favourable garments and made quite a success of herself, if not of her accent.

Madame came gliding back, glowing with pride and achievement. 'There's a gown but this day arrived which will make Madame the envy of everyone.'

Valma nodded, her eyes on the slender fair-haired girl who had parted the pale blue curtains at the end of the room and was advancing towards them with the typical mannequin's glide. The gown was lovely, pale ice blue satin, but after eyeing it critically, she shook her head.

Madame turned to Kerry inquiringly, but the girl also shook her head and, as if it had been a signal, the mannequin quietly slipped away.

'Ah, but no, the colour is not for Mademoiselle. It is something richer that is needed.' The pseudo-Frenchwoman glanced at Valma. 'But perhaps Mademoiselle is making her debut?'

'Miss Derwin is getting her trousseau,' Valma replied. 'She is to be married to Paul Devron.'

'To Paul Devron!' The rather calculating light eyes turned to Kerry with new respect. She sensed a worthwhile customer.

'Ah, mademoiselle, please accept my congratulations.' She turned briskly towards the curtains. 'Ginette, the Bronze Dawn.' As the curtains parted again and the fair-haired girl re-entered, this time wearing a black dress that was starkly simple except for a great sweep of silver train, she added: 'While Ginette is changing, perhaps you would care to examine Duet.'

Kerry had to restrain a desire to laugh aloud. It seemed absurd calling dresses by name, but even so there was a light of interest in her eyes as she looked at the black and silver dress. It was vaguely Grecian in appearance, off one shoulder and plainly sheathlike. From the single shoulder seam, narrow at the top and extremely full at the bottom, the silver drape fell in sinuous cascades, belted in at a trim, moulded waist.

'I like that,' she said decisively.

Valma gave her a doubtful look. 'It's a bit sophisticated for you,' she replied.

'Ah, but on Mademoiselle it would look exquisite.'

Valma glanced critically from the black and silver dress to Kerry, visualizing its striking simplicity on the younger girl, and then nodded.

'Try it on, then.'

Kerry gave a mental sigh of delight. She had bought her first evening dress. She had decided to have it already, even if she hadn't yet tried it on. It must fit. If it didn't, it could be altered.

Again the curtains parted. This time it was a dark-haired girl who entered, as the blonde slipped out, and the dress could only be the Bronze Dawn. The material was a heavy bronze velvet, simply cut, which Kerry adored on sight. However, she tried both on and also bought a tailored linen dress of dark brown and yellow. Valma, almost carelessly, as if her shopping spree had only been an excuse to help Kerry get her trousseau together, bought a couple of day dresses. When they eventually left the shop even Valma, good actress as she was, showed signs of pent-up mirth. Kerry could restrain herself no longer. Oblivious of passers-by, she burst out laughing.

'I didn't think people like that existed outside films and books.'

'I've met her type before.' Valma's lips quirked in an irrepressible smile. 'She undoubtedly has the best place in the district, but I nearly had hysterics on the other two occasions I went there.'

Kerry was silent on the return journey. Buying her new clothes seemed to bring her wedding to Paul nearer. She tried to imagine herself already married to him, alone with him in the little hunting lodge which he owned in the mountains. He had described the scene to her so vividly it was only too easy to visualize it now. There would be the vivid blue of the lake and the towering mountains, white-crested and remote. They would ring the little valley, shutting her in with Paul.

It was bewildering to be two Kerry Derwins, the new feminine Kerry who had realized on the drive to Exeter just how much Paul did mean to her and the remnants of the old scornful Kerry who had derided and also feared love. The derision was gone, but the fear still lingered to make her unsure and doubtfully apprehensive of the future. It would stab her suddenly in cold waves up her spine when she thought of her inexorably approaching wedding day, but it wasn't strong enough to gain ascendancy over her love for Paul. It could only torture her with a continual subconscious fear that would sometimes flare to the forefront of her mind. It could never win and one day, very soon, it would lose. Somehow she was confident of that.

CHAPTER NINE

KERRY's wedding day dawned bright and cheerful. The bride had spent an entirely sleepless night. She had watched the stars pale and the sun come up. She had lain stiff and taut and she had trembled.

Mallie's knock came on the door and Kerry shivered down into the protection of the covers, pretending to be asleep, as if she would ward off the events of the day.

Relentlessly Mallie pounded on the door again, then she opened it and came in. She was flustered and excited, but she held the breakfast tray she carried with extreme care.

Kerry saw it was no use pretending any longer and raised a white face from hiding in the pillow. Mallie clucked anxiously when she saw the strain on the young face.

'What's wrong, Kerry darling?'

Kerry swallowed hard. 'N-nothing,' she stammered. 'Just nerves.'

She knew it wasn't just nerves, though. During the night the old fears had grown and intensified a thousand times. All she wanted was to flee and hide. If there only had been a secret island in the bogs, the island of the witch girl Metani.

Mallie set the breakfast tray down on a small bedside table and Kerry gave it a look of distaste.

'I couldn't eat.'

'Don't be so foolish,' Mallie retorted sternly. 'We don't want you fainting when you walk down the aisle.'

'Anyway, I don't usually have breakfast in bed.'

'All brides-to-be have breakfast in bed.' Mallie backed towards the door and wagged an admonitory finger. 'Now you be good and eat it all up.'

Kerry forced a wan smile as Mallie went out. It was going back to childhood to be good and eat it up. She didn't feel like a child, though. Across the room hung the white satin of the dress she must put on in only a short time. She shivered and pushed the breakfast tray to the back of the table.

For a moment she lay back with her

hands clasped behind her head. However had she managed to get herself into this situation? Surely Kerry Derwin had sworn never to marry—but that had been before she met Paul Devron. She didn't understand her mind, or the muddled feelings of her body. All that was left was her old fear and an overwhelming compulsion that wouldn't let her draw back, a self-torture that mocked at her, yet forced her to go on.

She pushed back the covers impatiently and lowered her feet to the ground. Standing up, she ran slim fingers through her hair and crossed to the window. The grey moorlands seemed to stretch endlessly outside. But they weren't endless. The road reached Rylston, where Paul waited for her.

She tried to calm her mind, to force it off the future, to the past. There had been the farewell party of the film company. She had been happy there. Paul, darkly attractive in his gypsy dress, had driven across to pick her up. That night, at the request of the rest of the people, they had danced the famous gypsy dance of the film.

For a moment time did slip away. There was the exciting, heady music of the violins. The full, billowing folds of her skirt swirled around her. With a gay provocative laugh, she tossed her fiery-crowned head and her swift dancing feet took her out of reach of the gypsy. The violins screamed high and exultant. She was conscious as she danced of the lithe, pantherish grace of the man who was to be her husband. The tempo of the dance quickened. He was the hunter and she the hunted; but still a provocative quarry who was not unwilling to be caught. Strong hands caught her at last, caught and held her. The music slowed, became soft and sensuous. She was aware of Paul's dark, warm eyes holding hers and there was no laughter in them. Their steps slowed with the music. The magnetic attraction that had nothing to do with acting held them in thrall. The music died away in a soft, sibilant whisper, the lights dimmed, and as they did so Paul's lips touched hers, not passionately, but with the languorous and insinuating sensuality of the whispering music. Then the lights had gone up and they had been laughing and bowing to their audience.

Kerry sighed. If Paul made her feel like that, what did she fear?

She turned from the window and halfheartedly picked at the breakfast Mallie had brought her. It was half cold now and seemed absolutely tasteless, but she forced herself to eat it. It wouldn't do to faint in the middle of everything. She was proud, and even if she was afraid, she didn't intend to let anybody know it.

Mallie came back along the corridor and a little while later she heard the sound of running water. The footsteps returned and then a knock came at the door.

'I'm running your bath, Miss Kerry.'

'Thank you,' she called out, and was surprised to hear how calm her voice was.

She drew on a dressing-gown and went along to the bathroom. As she passed Rick's door, it suddenly opened. He looked older, with his dark clothes and slicked-back hair. There was a worried look in his eyes as he put out a hand to stop her.

'Kerry.'

She stopped and turned. She was still white, but the calmness that had been in her voice when she spoke to Mallie had settled over her face in a protective shield.

'What's the matter?'

'That's what I was going to ask.' He watched her and the frown grew. 'Kerry, he hasn't persuaded you to marry him against your will, has he?' He ran an embarrassed hand through his hair, spoiling its unusual neatness. 'I know Kel and I used to tease you about this sort of thing, but we . . . we wouldn't want . . .' He broke off as Kerry's fingers touched his arm momentarily.

'Thanks, Rick. Everything's all right. It's just nerves. I'm told nearly every bride gets them on her wedding day.'

When she came down the stairs later, a kind of numbness had descended on her. The gleaming folds of white satin whispered softly about her slender figure and her flaming hair was neatly arranged under the cobweb fineness of the lace veil. Her hands held the white bouquet with just the right amount of firmness. There was no feverish grip on it. She walked with poise and graceful dignity.

But there was no misty light of happiness in her eyes. Her face was aloof and her eyes had an unnatural calm. She was an automaton who had drunk of the waters of Lethe.

Her father and Mallie watched her advance. Both were beginning to feel anxiety. A jittery, or plainly scared, Kerry they could have understood and reassured, but this aloof stranger worried them.

It was a silent drive to Rylston and the church where they were to be married. After the ceremony they would go to the hotel where the reception was to be held and then on to London. The following morning a plane would take them to the large American airport where Paul had left his own craft. After that Paul himself would fly them to the little hunting lodge.

As they neared the church it was quite evident that large crowds had collected. Outside the church itself they were so thick that police had been called to keep the crowd in check and form a lane for the bridal party to enter. It was inevitable that the marriage of so popular a star as Paul Devron would attract attention.

Kerry alighted from the car at her father's side, still with that unnatural calm. Even when she saw Paul it didn't shatter. Only when his hand touched hers, sliding on the platinum eternity ring with its tiny sparkling diamonds that he had chosen after she had once half seriously said the plain gold band always reminded her of slave bands, did a strange tremor run through her. She heard the words of the minister, 'I pronounce that they be man and wife', in that same aloof calm.

Kerry Devron. It had a strange and frightening sound.

They went into the vestry and Kerry found herself signing her own name for the last time. When Paul kissed her the lips under his were cold and stiff. He didn't say anything, but his touch was gentle as he drew her hand up to rest on his arm.

The numbing calm was still on her as they went up the aisle together, the four bridesmaids behind them. One of them was Barbie, the other three more distant friends from Rylston. All four were too thrilled and excited to be aware of anything different about the bride. To them they were the bridesmaids at the wedding of Paul Devron. Although Kerry had been their friend for years, especially Barbie, for the moment they could only envy her and think how lovely she was, without seeing that her expression was not as a bride's should be.

Kerry and Paul entered the car and were driven to the reception. There the calm was still unbroken. She said what was expected of her, cut the magnificent cake and responded to the toasts with a poise that she didn't know she possessed, before saying her goodbyes as she and her new husband set off for the station.

They had a first-class compartment to themselves on the train to London, luckily, for there had been a strained atmosphere ever since the journey began, fifteen minutes ago. She felt the strain acutely, but if Paul also felt it, he gave no sign. All the time he had chatted amiably, not touching personal topics, but Kerry had answered in monosyllables.

When she turned and met his eyes, he smiled. 'Have you seen any rushes of the film yet?'

She made an effort to pull herself together. 'No.'

He jerked a quizzical eyebrow upwards. 'Pity. You should have done. Poor Valma said you quite eclipsed her.'

Her eyes opened wide. For a moment her panic was superseded by astonishment.

'I eclipse Valma!' She shook her head. 'I think she must have been imagining things, or being kind.'

Paul smiled again. 'Valma doesn't imagine things like that. She's quite jealous where her career is concerned.'

'Oh.' Kerry looked quite concerned. 'I didn't mean to. I mean I . . .'

He laughed and gently tweaked a lock of flaming hair. 'Of course you didn't. She doesn't mind in any case.'

'Does that mean Tom will give me another part?'

She sounded so excited that his laugh grew. 'So it's got you already! I told you it gets into your blood.'

She realized he was right. It was in her blood already, in so short a time. Even though, as he said, it was brittle and artificial, it had a strange charm.

A ghost of her old grin flashed out. 'I suppose it does. Do you think Tom will give me another part?' she repeated.

'You'll find it hard to get away from Tom,' he replied. 'He already has ideas about filming an old Greek legend. Do you think you could play one of the goddess Diana's huntresses?'

The grin grew until it had all its old mischievousness. 'I can use a bow and arrow,' she said, remembering the time when her aim had been better than even she had hoped. One year it had been the bow and arrows, the next year the Cossack stunt. Then for the first time her eyes had met and been held by the sparkling black ones of Paul Devron. Now she was his wife.

Abruptly the fear, waiting its chance in the background of her mind, came forward. The smile died and he saw the shadow cross her face. Quickly his smile also faded. They were sitting opposite each other, but before she could guess his intention, he crossed over to sit at her side and caught both of her hands in his, turning her to face him. Her eyes dropped before his and he spoke softly.

'Look at me, Kerry.' Very reluctantly she looked up. 'Why are you afraid of me? Is it because I'm your husband now?'

Kerry gasped and whitened. She tried to tug her hands free, but he held on to them. It was a firm but reassuring clasp. It told her how much he loved her, it spoke of desire and passion, but also of a great tenderness, and somehow brought a measure of peace to her confused mind. Why do you fear me? it seemed to say. I love you. She met his eyes and they said the same thing.

He smiled very slightly, pulling her gently towards him with his hold on her hands. He had to be so careful with her, this little wild creature who wasn't yet tamed to the hold of the hunter.

'Look at me,' he said, and his voice was

still soft. 'Am I such an ogre, Kerry?'

She looked at him, at the dark, attractive features, the warm black eyes that now held a whimsical smile, the tall lean body that had such a steel-hard strength, and in spite of her fear she felt her love rising in her. His consideration and understanding were other endearing factors. What other man would have been so patient with her childish fears?

She smiled herself, ashamedly. 'No, Paul.' Her voice was so low he had to lean forward to catch it. 'Just a stupid little coward.'

His lips brushed hers lightly, then he released her, but didn't shift back to his own side of the carriage.

During the long journey she managed to recapture some of the poise that had been hers during the reception, the automatic unnatural calm that at last made her able to carry on an impersonal conversation with a fair degree of equanimity. Of Paul's thoughts she had no knowledge. A strangely enigmatical expression had descended on his face.

At last they reached London and took a taxi to the hotel. It was large and luxurious and their feet sank into the thick pile of the carpets, muffling and silencing their tread. Their apartment looked out over the greenness of the park and was exquisitely furnished. In the centre of the soft blue carpet the two cases they had brought with them—the rest were already at the airport—looked lost and alone.

She crossed to a connecting door and looked in. It was a bedroom in yellow and brown. With a quickly beating heart and heightened colour, she quickly shut it again, hoping Paul hadn't noticed, but he was apparently staring out of the window at the park below.

Hearing the door snap shut, he turned to face her. 'Hungry?'

Glad of something prosaic to occupy her mind, she shook her head. 'Not very, but I would like some tea.'

He came away from the window and crossed towards her. 'Do you want it up here, or would you rather go downstairs?'

'Downstairs,' she answered quickly. It would be public there, plenty of people would be about. She couldn't face the thought yet of being alone with Paul in their apartment.

A short while later they went downstairs to where tea was being served and their conversation was still formal, almost like that of strangers. Afterwards they walked through the little park that was nearby, listened for a while to a band playing in the bandstand, then continued on until they came to the Embankment. There they leaned against the stone wall, looking down into the water. It flowed serenely. There was nothing turbulent about it, like there was about her life, Kerry thought. The river was sedate, if rather murky. A cheeky little tug chugged by on the other side, towing a heavily laden and cumbersome barge behind it. Both of them watched it in silence, then walked on further.

In front of them something towered up into the sky. 'Cleopatra's Needle,' Kerry said, remembering it from her other visit to London years ago.

'Only it wasn't built by Cleopatra,' said Paul with a faint smile.

She gave him a quick glance of surprise. 'Then why do they call it that?'

He shrugged. 'Heaven knows. I forget who really built it.'

She stared at the strange hieroglyphics on the slender, towering needle with moody eyes. This thing of the ancient past seemed to reduce her own troubles to small petty things. The colourful procession of life had gone by it for thousands of years. It had the calm, impervious arrogance of something that had watched the centuries go by and impulsively she reached out and touched it. Some of the calm seemed to flow into her and for a time she was at peace as they turned to go back to the hotel.

Once back in the hotel suite, her nerves began to jangle at the edge of the calm, but she managed to control them fairly well, for the time being.

When it was time to dress for dinner she pulled on the black dress with its silver drape and for a long moment stood looking at herself in the mirror. It moulded her slender figure to perfection, giving her an unusual air of sophistication and the silver drape swept in shimmering folds to her feet, held in at the waist by the narrow black belt.

Paul came in from the adjoining dressing room, slim and attractive in a well-cut dinner jacket. His eyes went over her head with a light of appreciation in them and he crossed the room slowly to her. His hands went up on either side of her face, the long fingers twining themselves in the soft, fine hair.

'You're very lovely, Kerry Devron.'

She shivered under his touch. Kerry Devron. It had the sound of possessiveness.

He released her and held out his arm. 'Shall we go down?'

Silently she placed her hand on his arm. Afterwards she never knew what they had for dinner that night. They danced to the strains of a perfect orchestra, but her body had a tautness against him and the old enjoyment of the dance was absent. She was too strung up and nervy, and tiredness was beginning to make her limbs feel heavy.

As they returned to their table, Paul glanced down at her. 'Tired?'

She wanted to deny it, to prolong the time before she must return upstairs, but her eyelids drooped heavily belying the emphatic shake of her head.

'Yes you are,' he contradicted, and stood up. 'Off you go. I have to see about checking out in the morning.'

Reluctantly, Kerry rose to her feet. With his hand lightly beneath her elbow, she crossed to the foot of the stairs. There he left her and she mounted slowly, opening the door of their suite with fingers that trembled. When they touched the door of the brown and yellow room, they were shaking so violently she couldn't control them.

She sat down on the stool at the dressing table, laid her hands on the polished surface and looked at them. Gradually, by force of will, their trembling lessened, but they still quivered as she rose to her feet again and unfastened the narrow black belt of her dress.

A little later she heard Paul in the adjoining dressing room and when he knocked on the door she stood in the middle of the floor, a pale green quilted dressing gown belted closely about her, a froth of white peeping from beneath it.

She stiffened and tried to speak, but her voice seemed to have gone from her. An awful dryness constricted her throat and clammy coldness shivered through her.

He knocked again, then after a moment turned the handle and entered. His purple dressing gown emphasized his darkness and his eyes dropped to her feet, where the froth of white material showed.

He came nearer and the smile in his eyes grew warmer. 'You're very lovely, Kerry,' he said, as he had earlier, but there was a new note in his voice, a note that made her dig her fingernails into the palms of her hands.

She remained quite passive as he reached out and drew her close to him, but as he bent his head to kiss her she came suddenly to life.

'No, Paul! No!' Her back arched with a violent movement of withdrawal from him and she beat at his chest with small, frantic fists. 'Let me go! Oh, please let me go!'

'Kerry.' He released her and put a hand to her, but she shrank away from it. 'Don't look at me like that, child,' he cried out in uncontrollable pain. 'You've nothing to fear from me. I love you.'

* * *

Kerry awoke in the morning with dark shadows under her eyes. She hadn't thought she would sleep at all, but complete exhaustion, combined with the fact that she hadn't slept the night before, had sent her at last into a black oblivion that was more than sleep.

She awoke slowly, as if reluctant to come back to reality, surprised to find herself refreshed. The tiredness of the day before had gone, but not its problems. There was still her marriage to Paul. Even she knew they couldn't go on like last night.

She went through into the adjoining bathroom and stood under a stinging cold shower to try to pull herself together. Slightly numbed, she rubbed herself dry and dressed in the grey travelling suit.

When she went through the brown and yellow room into the second room of the suite, there was a table laid for two. Paul was standing by the window, but he turned as she came in. He saw her hesitation and waved a hand towards the table.

'Eat first. We'll talk afterwards.'

She moved slowly towards the table, trying to read his expression, but it was unreadable in its very normality. He was too good an actor for her to guess what he might be thinking underneath.

She sat down at the table and started to pick at the daintily laid breakfast, feeling as if it would choke her. She wished she could imitate Paul, who seemed quite at ease, not talking too much or too quickly, just dropping a casual remark every now and again into the silence. She sipped sweet, strong coffee, watching him unobtrusively, while the other hand clenched in her lap.

As she finished the coffee and put down the cup, he looked towards her with a smile.

'More coffee?' His voice was as casual as if they had breakfasted together for years.

She nodded. 'Please,' she murmured, and watched him pour the steaming black liquid into her cup. When she was absently about to put the fourth spoonful of sugar into it, he reached across and caught her wrist.

'You've already put three in, Kerry.'

She felt the strength of his fingers on her wrist, halting her hand, and wondered if he would use that strength against her if she sent him from her again.

There was silence until they had both finished their coffee. Finally Paul rose to his feet and crossed to the padded window seat.

'Come over here, Kerry.'

With lagging footsteps she obeyed and sat down at his side. Her eyes, wide and apprehensive, were raised to his face and then quickly dropped to the hands clenched convulsively together in her lap.

'You know we can't go on like we did last night, don't you?' he said at last, very quietly.

She nodded, without speaking. Momentarily her eyes raised to his again, then as swiftly dropped. His had been tender and understanding and she hated herself for her cowardice.

'Why did you marry me?' he asked softly.

She hesitated, yet had to be truthful. 'Because I love you,' she answered without looking up.

'And last night?'

'I was afraid.' Still she wouldn't look at him.

'Yet that other time, in the cave, when I asked you to marry me, you weren't afraid when I kissed you.' He saw her upward startled glance that remembered the difference of those other kisses and laughed with a soft triumph. 'Yes, Kerry. I could have anticipated our marriage then and you wouldn't have fought me. Why are you afraid of me now?' But still she wouldn't answer him and he sighed and stood up. 'I suppose it's my own fault really. From the moment I realized I'd fallen in love with you, at the ball, I very deliberately did everything I could to make you love me, without giving you a chance to grow up.' He tugged gently at her hand and made her stand up too. 'Don't worry, child. It's my own fault for rushing things. I'm afraid I very unscrupulously manoeuvred you on more than one occasion. I shall have to be patient now, but one day you'll have to grow up and get over these absurd fears—and they are absurd,' he added with a slight smile. 'If you remembered back clearly to that day in the cave, you would realize it.' She stood hesitantly before him, uncertain what to say or do, and he turned her gently towards the other room. 'Now you'd better finish packing. We've a plane to catch.'

* * *

The blue water lapped gently at the grassy, wooden slopes that led down to it. Kerry, dressed in slacks and a light blouse, stood looking at it moodily, her hands thrust into her pockets.

It was three days and two nights since they had arrived at the lodge, which was Paul's Canadian home. On both those nights Paul had wished a courteous goodnight at her door. She was feeling vaguely disappointed now, yet fearful. There was a quiet beauty about the moonlit sky and the dark shapes of the tall mountains surrounding the valley. There was also a wild primitive call about them.

They struck a deep, echoing response within her, that shivered through her, laughing at her fear. She wanted Paul at her side, yet she was apprehensive of standing with him in the quiet moonlight where they would be the only living things for miles. She wanted his kisses, he hadn't touched her since they left London, yet she still feared the consummation of their marriage.

As if her thoughts had brought him there, Paul appeared at her side.

'It's beautiful, isn't it?' he said softly.

Kerry nodded. 'Lovely,' she agreed.

He suddenly left her and bent down in the tall grasses and brush some yards away. She watched him surprised, then saw him pushing a small Indian canoe into the water. When he beckoned to her, she came to him curiously.

'On a night like this you have to look around from the centre of the lake, Kerry. It's something you'll never forget.'

He helped her into the canoe and she felt the familiar thrill his touch gave her. Why then did she fear?

Neither of them spoke as he paddled them out to the centre of the lake. There, still in silence, they remained perfectly motionless. Gradually the ripples produced by their coming died away and they were alone in a dreaming world. The surface of the lake was like a magic mirror, strange creatures of myth and fairytale could have emerged from it. The mountains thrust their snowcapped peaks into the star-studded sky, gleaming in the moonlight, aloof and apart from the world of humanity. The strange lilting voices of ethereal creatures should echo down those distant slopes in cadences from a realm not known to man.

Kerry felt the brooding silence affecting her strangely. It shivered along her nerves and set her heart beating quickly. Without turning her head, she knew Paul had looked round at one particular mountain.

'That's Lokara,' he said in a soft voice that didn't disturb the quiet. 'The Indians say that beneath it somewhere sleep the bodies of the young braves who tried to capture the immortal snow maiden that lives on the peak. They don't try now, either because they know it's useless, or else they've become modernized,' he said with a trace of cynicism.

'What happened to the braves?'

'Whenever one of them catches sight of the snow maiden, he must pursue her, and always she sends an avalanche down on him. White men have climbed the mountains and have come back, but the Indians will go no further than where the snow starts on Lokara. They fear they may see the snow maiden and anyone who sees her must pursue her to death. She has the pale skin of the snows and her black hair glitters with ice crystals. Her eyes are the cold green of the glaciers. Some of them have come back to the village after catching a brief glimpse of her on the lower slopes, but always they have had to go back to seek her. The last time it happened was nearly fifty years ago. He escaped from the snow fall she sent down on him and returned to the village, like some of the others, but the next day he went back to the mountain and was never seen again.'

'Perhaps he found her,' Kerry suggested.

'Perhaps.' There was a faint tinge of bitterness in his voice. 'It's unlikely. He probably lies buried somewhere beneath the weight of ice and snow she sent upon him.'

She went silent, sensing something in his words that was directed at her. She didn't feel like a snow maiden though. All her nerves were thrilling in a most peculiar way and she wished she had never come out on the lake.

'Can we go back now?' she asked.

'Certainly.' His voice was normal again. She wasn't to know that beneath his forced calm the same peculiar torture was jangling his nerves and that only a small spark would precipitate it into an exploding volcano.

When they reached the shore he jumped out and pulled the canoe further on to the shore, then helped her out. While she stood in the long grass, looking out over the lake, he lifted the canoe right out of the water and replaced it in its original position.

'Well, did you like it?' His voice was slightly harsh, but somehow that didn't warn her. She was too occupied with her own stirred senses.

She turned to face him as he straightened up by the side of the canoe. 'It was lovely. Once at home we arranged to go rowing on a stream at night time. Rick made himself sick eating too much. Kel and I went alone and . . .'

Abruptly she broke off. Too late, she realized that this of all nights, she shouldn't have mentioned Kelvin's name.

Paul gave a strangled exclamation and in

a single savage movement caught her by the shoulders.

'Kerry, are you completely inhuman? How dare you mention Kelvin Treveryl's name at a time like this?'

His grip on her shoulders was hurting her and she moved ineffectually under his hands.

'Paul, you're hurting me!'

'So I'm hurting you,' he snapped, and shook her violently. 'How much do you think you've hurt me? Do you think I enjoy seeing you shrink from me? It's about time I stopped treating you as a child. You won't grow up on your own.'

He bent his head and pressed his lips savagely to hers. Kerry tried to push him away, feeling her senses reeling. His grip tightened on her, bruising her whole body. She struggled with him desperately. Through the thin material of the blouse his hands burned into her back. Once she managed to break away from him, but he pulled her roughly back and swept her right up into his arms. Holding her high against him, he strode to the door of the lodge and jerked it open with his shoulder.

Although she knew the room so well already, that night printed it indelibly on her memory. The wooden walls with their Indian souvenirs, the wooden floor, kept polished and clean by the old half-breed Indian woman who came up from the village in the forest, the vaguely Grecian couch piled with cushions placed before the great log fire blazing in the hearth. There was other furniture in the room, but it was hidden in the flickering shadows thrown by the fire and the lamps hadn't yet been lit.

He stalked across the room and ungently threw her down among the cushions and stood over her, tall and frightening. His eyes were smouldering dangerously and as she tried to shrink down among the cushions he laughed as he watched her. With an incredibly swift movement he was suddenly sitting by her side, leaning over her, as he had on the Roman film set. But this was reality. Her body was bruised with the strength of his arms and her lips throbbed with the savage kisses pressed on them.

His touch was like fire on her bare skin and she gasped as his hands caressed her with an insidious sensualism.

'Paul!' Her cry was almost an entreaty, but he heard a new note running through it and laughed.

Something ran through her that was mad and wild. The languor and the sharp painful excitement she had felt that day in the cave had suddenly come back a thousand times intensified. Her fingers gripped his shoulders and the desire that was in him suddenly became an exquisite agony in her also that demanded satisfaction.

Paul laughed again, but this time it was differently. She heard the exultant triumph in it and didn't care, not even when he rose to his feet with her still in his arms and crossed the room to where the dark shadows waited beyond the flickering firelight.

* * *

When the knock came on the door, Kerry didn't stir. She still slept, her flaming hair spread over the pillow and a tiny smile on her lips.

Very softly the door opened and Paul entered. He was dressed in riding clothes and carried a small tray with tea on it, which he set down carefully on the little bedside table.

Kerry stirred as he leaned over her and

opened her eyes to find the warm dark ones of her husband smiling at her. She smiled back sleepily and lifted one arm to link around his neck. Their kiss was long and satisfying and left both happily content.

'Forgiven?' he whispered.

'Absolutely.'

As he straightened up she saw the tray and lifted herself up on one elbow.

'Tea.'

He handed her the cup and his eyes rested on the frothy white material of the nightdress.

'That garment is positively indecent!'

Kerry grinned. 'That's what I said when Valma gave it to me as a wedding present.' She looked at his riding clothes. 'Are we going riding?'

'If you want to.'

'I didn't know you had any horses here.' Her eyes sparkled in anticipation. 'You know I love riding.'

'They're down at the Indian village. They take care of them for me while I'm away.'

Pushing back the covers, she padded over to the window on bare feet and looked out. There she yawned and stretched luxuriously.

'It looks lovely out. I feel like riding.'

'Then if you want to go, you'd better put on something more substantial than that.' He came up behind her and slipping his arms around her waist, drew her up against him and dropped a light kiss on her hair. 'And if you're concerned about your immediate safety, you'd better take protective measures right now or you might bring out the beast in me,' he added.

Kerry turned in his arms with a chuckle. 'I like both you and the beast.'

His expression altered abruptly as he looked down at her and she saw a small frown draw his dark brows together.

'Kerry, I apologize for last night. I was a brute.'

She smiled and leaned her head against him. 'No, you weren't,' she contradicted. 'I was a silly little idiot. Anyway, I can't work up the least bit of anger, so I'm not going to try.'

In retrospect, she now realized that beneath her fear she had enjoyed every moment of his brutal treatment of her. There was something wonderfully satisfying and thrilling in being conquered by the strength of the man she loved.

He released her and went over to the

door. 'I'll get the horses while you're getting dressed.'

Some time later, dressed in the familiar black jodhpurs and black tunic that Rylston knew so well, she came out into the adjoining room.

Paul took her hand to pull her outside to where two wiry piebald ponies waited.

'You'll find them a bit different from Smoky,' he warned. 'They're fresh too.'

Kerry vaulted into the saddle and immediately the pony started to buck. Her teeth flashed in a delighted grin.

'You monkey,' she said softly, and very expertly took him in hand. The pony, surprised to find that the figure on his back was so completely in control of the situation, despite its slight weight, gave up the unequal battle.

And, side by side, they rode together down the trail and into the forest.

Photoset, printed and bound in Great Britain by
REDWOOD BURN LIMITED, Trowbridge, Wiltshire